A PINCH OF WHIMSY
AND
A DASH OF WEIRD

For Shelly,
with thanks for all
your kindness and support.
Always look within...

Barb

A PINCH OF WHIMSY
AND
A DASH OF WEIRD

PLUS

THE COMFORT OF GERANIUMS,
A NOVELLA

BARBARA MEGIE LARKIN

To order additional copies of this book, contact:
Xlibris Corporation
1-888-795-4274
www.Xlibris.com
Orders@Xlibris.com
28167

CONTENTS

DEDICATION

For my mother and father, with love always and forever.
And for my grandmother, my light.

THE POSSIBILITY OF
MERCY TYLDEN

Marley was dead: to begin with.
There is no doubt whatever about that.

Charles Dickens
A Christmas Carol

Last summer while on a two-week holiday in London, I met a delightful English woman named Mercy Tylden. This lady had a profound effect on my life, and I will never forget her or cease being grateful to her. We became acquainted over lunch one day in the Crypt Café. I don't know how familiar you might be with London, but this café is located underneath the church of St. Martin-in-the-Fields, just across from Trafalgar Square. Though the lighting tends to be on the dim side, the place has both a sacred and charming atmosphere all its own. I'd bet that many of the tourists who straggle in from a long morning's tour of the city never realize that they're having their lunch over dead people, long since gone. People who once lived and struggled and worked and loved and died a couple of centuries ago. Now only faint tracings remain of their names and dates on the crypts, and those are covered over with tables and chairs for today's diners.

Some might find this a little morbid, a little creepy, but I didn't. It was quiet and dark and cool down there, a refuge from the battering noise of the London streets above. There is also a museum gift shop and a brass-rubbing center, and it's always busy. When I'm in London, I try to eat there at least once or twice a week. I have my favorite table. It's up against one of the arches and directly under a small spotlight, so I can sit over a leisurely, inexpensive meal and read and write, or simply sit there and think. On this visit, however, I had been so busy with sightseeing that I didn't make it to the café until the first week had passed. As I came in, I saw that "my" table was vacant and waiting for me.

And that's how I came to meet Mercy Tylden. That is, I didn't so much "meet" her as—I have no choice but to be blunt. She was one of the many souls buried below those crypts, and my table was situated directly over her resting place.

I have no doubt lost some of my audience at this point, but I do assure you that Mercy Tylden was real. Not real in terms of physical body-ness, but real in her spiritual presence, real in her soul. And I came, in time, to love her and understand why she chose me to—but that comes later in my story. For all the skeptics out there, I admit to having been an imaginative child. "Full of strange fancies," as one of my teachers put it. And in my fifty-odd years of living, I have never lost that fancifulness. I have learned to let myself be open to all the possibilities that might exist; the possibilities of what God is and what He sends us; the possibilities of what lies just beneath our earthly shells. Some might call this my inner voice. Whatever it is, I have always tried to listen to it and be guided by it, and it has never led me wrong.

Mercy was not the first spiritual being I had ever experienced. I sensed the soul of my father a few weeks after his death. I was in my house when it happened, paying bills one afternoon, when an eerie sensation washed over me, starting at my head and flowing down my entire body. I stopped in the middle of writing a check, and the words "Oh— Dad's here" involuntarily popped out of my mouth. It wasn't frightening. It was very natural. His presence didn't, perhaps couldn't, stay long, but I'm certain that he was there because he wanted to make sure I was all right. Still the worrywart, my dad, protective of me in death as well as in life. That experience reassured me and taught me to keep looking for and believing in all the possibilities that are.

Well, that's a long lead-in to what happened the day Mercy Tylden made herself known to me. I was sitting at my usual table, finishing a vegetarian quiche and reading *Sense and Sensibility*, when—it suddenly was there, that same feeling I'd had when Dad came to me. I stayed very still, trying to sense who and where it was. It didn't feel like my father. No, somehow I knew it was a female presence. Maybe my grandmother? I'd lost her when I was only 18, and had grieved for her ever since. The last time I'd been with her, I had told her I loved her as I left, and it had always troubled me since then, whether she had heard me or not. As I continued to be still, the feeling went away, but the spiritual presence did not. It was strong and all around me. I waited for something, anything to happen. Nothing. Five minutes passed, and I was beginning to think I was wrong. But finally I whispered, "Is there someone here?"

I heard no actual voice, saw no actual person, but from somewhere deep inside me—my heart?—I sensed a woman speaking to me.

"Yes," she said. "*I* am. Do you believe I am here?"

I began to sweat a little. Maybe I was having a dream, but I answered the voice.

"Um—yes, I can feel you. Do I know you? Who—who are you, and where are you, please?"

"My name is—was—Mercy Tylden. And I am with you, here in this place, though my body lies just beneath your feet."

Ok, time for the dream to be over. Time to wake up. I slammed my book shut and got up from the table. My heart was hammering away in my chest, and I was afraid I might faint.

"Do not you be afraid. I am no one to fear. Please. Please to be seated again, and allow me to be with you."

"Are you really—real?" I asked shakily. (I was an English major in college, and that's the best I could come up with?)

"Why do you doubt your senses? What evidence would you have of my reality, beyond that of your senses?"

"Because," I began, "Because a little thing affects them. You might be . . ." Then I knew it was no dream. "Wait a minute, this sounds like . . . that's from Dickens—*A Christmas Carol!*"

I laughed in spite of my fear and surprise. I felt her laugh along with me. At least I now knew that when we leave this world, we take our senses of humor along with us.

Ok, I thought. *This is real. This is not just a fragment of an underdone potato. This is really happening, and is another gift from God, another possibility, so don't blow it.*

What should I say next? I didn't want to just sit there and have it look like I was talking to myself, though I see plenty of people in London (especially on the Underground) doing the same thing, and nobody pays them any mind. I may be open to new experiences, but I'm still self-conscious, so I opened my book again and made a great show of reading and taking notes.

Mercy had picked up my thoughts.

"Nor am I a blot of mustard," she said gaily. "You need not use your mouth to speak. If you please, you may converse with me in your mind. That is, if you wish to speak to me."

I looked around the café. Sometimes in these old places, acoustics can play strange tricks on the ear, and I still wanted to be sure I wasn't the victim of a prank. As I glanced about, my eyes stopped on a man, a quite nice-looking man, actually, about my age, who was sitting a few tables away. He returned my gaze for a moment, and then smiled at me. A very charming smile, too. It was nice to know that at my age, I could still provoke smiles like that in men. And did I mention he was good-looking, too? It almost made me forget that I was sitting at my table with a ghost.

Hold on, I thought. *Don't get distracted.* But I did take a moment to smile back at him. He reminded me of someone, I couldn't think who, but it would come to me later.

I gave my attention to Mercy.

"All right," I 'thought' at her, "I will try to talk to you with my mind. Can you understand me?"

"Oh, yes, your words and thoughts are very clear indeed."

"Well—that's good, then. You said your name is Mercy—?"

"Tylden."

"Mercy Tylden. Um. It's very nice to meet you, Mercy Tylden. My name is—"

"Oh, I have the honor of already knowing your name. I learnt it from your mind. Do I—shall I—may I call you Mrs. Gibson?"

"Well, actually, it's *Ms.* Gibson. I am divorced and I kept my married name. But please call me by my first name, Lucy."

"'Miz'?" She sounded puzzled.

"It's spelled *Ms.*, but we pronounce it 'Miz,'" I said. "I'll explain it all later. And how shall I address you?"

"If you please, call me Mercy."

"All right, Mercy. Did you wish to tell me anything? I mean, is there a reason . . . I'm sorry, I'm babbling, I'm just so bewildered and surprised and . . . though if there is any place in London where a spirit might likely come to me, this would be it."

"Yes, I have made myself known to you on purpose. That part is to come—I will 'explain it all later,' as you put it. But first, I am certain that you must have questions you wish to ask me."

Did I have questions? I was afraid if I began, I'd never stop. I didn't want it to sound like small talk at a cocktail party, but I did have a strong curiosity—no, tell the truth, Lucy, I was dying (no pun intended) to ask her about who she was and why she was here with me now.

"If you won't be offended, Mercy," I said, "I would like to know everything, at least everything you would care to tell me. When and where you were born, about your family, were you married, who was your husband—"

She interrupted me gently.

"Lucy, that is enough to cover several hours of conversation! But I am not offended, indeed, I am touched by your kind interest in me. I am not used to such—But I will tell you all I can about my life and myself. To begin with, I was born in Holborn, quite a distance, you know, from London in those days . . ."

I don't know how long I sat there "listening" to her, but the noise of dishes being clattered together, of chairs scraping on the floor, of people coming and going all fell away as I heard her story. All I could hear was her voice.

As she had begun to tell me, she was born in Holborn in 1775, and died at the age of 48 in 1823.

I had to stop her.

"Oh, you were born the same year as Jane Austen!"

"I do not believe I have ever heard of such a person," she said.

"Why, she's my favorite author. I'm sure you must have read *Pride and Prejudice* in your lifetime. Or this book I have with me now, *Sense and Sensibility*. She wrote several others."

"I never knew the name of the author of those books until now. In my day, the author's name was given as "By a Lady."

I asked without thinking.

"Did you ever happen to—" Fortunately, I stopped myself in time. *Dear God*, I thought, *I was actually going to ask her if she had ever run into Jane Austen. You have an incredible opportunity to ask Mercy questions, so for goodness' sake, at least ask intelligent ones!*

Well, just one more. I couldn't help it.

"If you died in 1823, Mercy, how did you know to quote from Dickens' *A Christmas Carol*?

"I pick up small bits of knowledge from others' minds from time to time. It amuses me, and does not hurt them. They never know that I am doing it."

I asked her pardon for my silly questions, and begged her to go on.

She came from a good and fairly prosperous family. Her father was the rector of a small parish in Holborn. He and his wife had eight children, and Mercy was the eldest.

"I was named for my dear grandmother, my father's mother. Sadly, she departed this life when I was quite young, and I have but dim memories of her. I do remember how fond she was of me, though, and whenever I entered a room where she was, her eyes were always bright with love for me."

"You sound sad, Mercy."

"Yes, I am, whenever I think of her. How I wish I could have known her as I grew older. Perhaps if I had had the benefit of her advice, things would have been different for me. I like to fancy sometimes that I was a particular favorite of hers."

"I'm sure it was no fancy, and that she loved you very much."

"Thank you for that, my dear. That comforts me."

She began to speak again, and I resolved not to interrupt anymore.

In addition to being rector, her father also had a day school for boys. He taught Greek and Latin, geography and all the classical poets and writers. Her mother, when she could take the time from her young family, taught reading and writing.

"I was most fortunate," Mercy said, "that my parents held liberal views about their daughters' education. My sisters and I were welcomed into my father's classroom, and had complete access to his extensive library. Those of us who wished to, could learn and read anything the boys did. It was an unusual thing for girls to acquire such an education, I believe. Indeed, my father seemed rather proud of the way I could hold my own against the boys, whether it were Virgil, history, or Shakespeare. But then, he was an excellent teacher, as was my dear mother."

Mercy's childhood was a happy one. They lived in a large, sunny rectory, which boasted a small orchard and garden. The children were all hearty and healthy, and their parents encouraged physical exercise. She described how she and her siblings spent many an hour running in between and around the apple trees, rolling down the hillocks in back of their home, and playing a game that sounded a lot like our own "hide-and-go-seek."

But in time, as their father's duties and responsibilities to his family, parishioners, and students increased, he found it necessary to take on a curate. One young man was highly praised and recommended by some mutual friends, and after several conversations with Mercy's father, it was decided. He was to be the new curate, and would live with the family.

"His name was Hugh Tylden," Mercy said. "And the day that he knocked on our door and presented himself to us was the day my childhood ended."

*   *   *

I lay awake for a long time that night in my hotel room, thinking over what I had experienced in the café that day. A part of me still insisted it had been a dream, or an hallucination brought on by jet lag, but I knew—I *knew*, deep inside myself, that Mercy Tylden was real, that we had talked, and that we had become like sisters in just a few short hours. And I couldn't get out of my mind the story she had shared with me about Hugh Tylden . . .

She described him to me as "charming" and "strikingly handsome" more than once. He had thick, black hair and piercing blue eyes. Though he was somewhat short, he was powerfully built.

"He had a wonderful ability to put people at their ease, and could talk on nearly any subject you could think of with wit and intelligence. He had a ready laugh, but could also compassionate with a grieving family who had lost a loved one. He was altogether a very pleasing young man."

Mercy's voice trailed away for a moment, then she began again.

"You must remember, dear Lucy, that I was only sixteen years old at the time, and had had but little experience with men outside of my family. I was quiet and rather shy, and would much prefer to listen than to speak. So, suddenly being in company with such a self-assured man as Hugh—he was eight years older than I, you know—and he appeared to be such a gentleman of the world and a man of God—well, my head was soon in a fair way to be turned. I couldn't help it. And in spite of my youth and inexperience, I did begin to think that on more than one occasion, he seemed to be paying me a good deal of attention. A very particular sort of attention. I liked him very much indeed, and to actually believe that he was returning that feeling—to put it simply, Lucy, what began as mere acquaintance quickly grew into a strong, mutual, and reciprocated love. We became secretly engaged."

I know Mercy wouldn't have known about, or even understood, what we now call "chemistry," but it was obvious to me that she and Hugh had felt an immediate physical, emotional, and yes, sexual attraction to each other, though I thought better of telling her this. But I understood very well, all too well, what she was talking about.

Mercy went on with her tale.

For form's sake, Hugh did not go to her father to ask for her hand until three months had passed. Her parents were very much surprised by the suddenness of their engagement, and expressed concern about Mercy's youth. But as they observed how devoted and attached the couple were, they gave their permission, only asking that they wait to marry until Mercy became seventeen. As they came to know their potential son-in-law better, they were convinced that Mercy could not be in better hands.

"I was so happy then," she said. I thought I could sense tears in her voice. "Hugh was like an angel to me, and his being older reassured me that he would always be there to guide and comfort me and stand between me and the uncertainties of this life. That I would be forever first in his heart, and in a safe harbour in his love, I never doubted for a moment. We would love each other, be married, bring up the children that God might in His grace send us, and I trusted that that was how it would ever be."

They were married the day after her seventeenth birthday.

She said earlier that she had appeared to me on purpose. I thought I knew what it might be, so I asked her if she had been happy in her marriage.

She remained silent for so long that I thought I might have presumed too much, and that she had left me. Then I suddenly felt her spirit more powerfully than ever, and she shocked me by crying out, "No! No! No! I was *not* happy! I cannot describe to you how *miserable* I was. I only thank God that we had no children to witness what I went through. This, this is the reason I have made myself known to you, Lucy. I have never told anyone about my life with Hugh, not even my own dear family. I was too ashamed, too embarrassed, too frightened to say anything. I know you better than you realize, Lucy, so I know you will understand me when I tell you that not long after Hugh and I were wed, I became 'clumsy'—'awkward'—'graceless.' Whenever anyone remarked on a bruise I had, I said I had fallen down the steps. Or walked into a door in the dark. Or struck my hip against a table. My horse threw me, that was why I broke my arm. I was limping because I had twisted my ankle while tending to the garden. I made sport of myself, deprecating myself for being so stupidly careless. You are the first person to ever hear this, Lucy, and I know from your mind that you were— 'clumsy,' too, in your marriage. Though we are centuries apart in age, we are truly sisters under the shadows of our marriages."

As I listened to her ever-increasing rage, I was becoming enraged, too. Angry beyond words at the abusers, the batterers, the cowards who only strike where the mark won't show. Angry at the ones who pierce our hearts with killing words. Angry at the men who profess to love us, then hammer away at our bodies and minds, until the strong, proud women we used to be begin to splinter and disintegrate. And finally, angry at those who beg our forgiveness and promise to never do it again, only to break that promise over and over again.

Yes, I knew exactly what Mercy was talking about, I knew why she had chosen me to tell her story to, because I myself had married such a one as Hugh Tylden.

Mercy and I sat in silence for a few minutes. I could feel her distress and my anger mingling inside my head and heart. I was the first to speak.

"I am sorry, so sorry, that you had to go through all of that, Mercy. You didn't deserve it. No woman deserves to be treated that way, and no normal man behaves like that. I hope to God you understand that you did nothing to provoke your abuse."

"But, you see, Lucy, he always told me he would not have had to do those—things to me, if I had been a better wife to him and obeyed him. He convinced me that I was ignorant and stupid, a careless housekeeper, and a cold, unaffectionate wife. How, in God's name, *could* I be affectionate with such a wicked man? It was my fault, he said, that we never had children. And he said he would continue to 'correct' my wrong behavior until I changed—or until I was dead. It was all the same to him. If I cried when he raged at me, he would promise to give me something worse to cry about. If I fought back—and at first, I tried to, I really did—well, he was stronger and louder than I, and it still ended in a beating. When I threatened to expose him to my parents and the church, he laughed and said no one would believe me. And upon reflection, that was probably the only true thing he said. He was a curate, a man of the cloth, and people looked up to and respected him. He could put on a pleasant, smiling countenance when he was in church and in company. But only I knew what lay beneath that charming exterior. He was evil, truly evil."

I knew from my historical reading about those days that as soon as a woman married, her money and any property she had legally became her husband's. The woman herself was considered property. She could not initiate a divorce suit. If she left her husband, she was immediately homeless and destitute. And of course, the scandal of her leaving meant she could no longer be received among "decent" people. If a woman married badly, there was nothing for her to do but accept her fate. Bad times, indeed, back then.

I realized how lucky I was to be living in this time. My abuser had told me I was stupid, too, and had me believing it. I also was slapped and kicked, but thank God, I'd never had any broken bones like Mercy had. After too, too many years of putting up with such a life, and with the help of a wonderful therapist and my attorney, I divorced him. That was a decade ago, and it has only been in the last four or five years that I have completely healed from the inside out. He didn't win that round. *I* did.

Now Mercy had chosen me to tell her story to, and I wanted to comfort her and thank her.

"Mercy," I said, "I'm so grateful that you trusted me enough to tell me these things. You have done me a great honor. And you are right, he *was* evil, and the sad thing is, men like that rarely change. They only get worse. Thank God, that we are both free of them now. I hope you understand that everything he did, everything he said, was done to hide his own shortcomings and insecurities. And I hope you are not thinking, 'if only I had—' There was nothing you could have done to stop his abusive behavior. Nothing. It was all him. And you were his unfortunate victim."

"Yes, I am coming to know all these things, Lucy, and you are helping me. To know your own story strengthens me and makes me feel closer to you. But I am afraid I have wearied you, my friend. You must leave now, go out and see the town or walk in one of the parks. But—will you please come back tomorrow?"

"Of course I will. Nothing would give me more pleasure. Tomorrow, then?"

"Tomorrow, dear Lucy."

As I walked toward the exit, I had to pass by the man who had smiled at me earlier. He was still there, and still smiling. As I approached, he stood up and said, "I hope you won't think me impertinent, but I have been watching you. That must be a most interesting book you're reading."

I laughed and said that it was, it was endlessly fascinating.

"My name is Richard Grayson," he said, and held out his hand.

And what could I do but take it?

"I'm Lucy Gibson. It's nice to meet you."

"Do you come here often? Oh dear, I'm sorry," he laughed. "That's about the worst pick-up line I could have chosen. Forgive me, please."

Pick-up line? I thought. *He's flirting with me!* It had been a long time, but I could still recognize it. I think I may even have blushed a little.

I told him that yes, I would be here the next day.

"Good," he said. "So maybe I'll see you then?"

"Yes, very likely you will."

"Good," he said again. "Well, it's been *very* nice talking with you."

I made what I thought was a graceful exit, and when I got outside, I crossed the street to the National Portrait Gallery. What a day I'd had! First an encounter with a spiritual being, then with an earthly one. Richard Grayson. *Odd that both our last names end in—son*, I thought. Nice manners, too. I'm always impressed by manners. As I entered the Gallery, I wondered what in the world tomorrow would bring.

*   *   *

I was uncomfortably conscious that my time in London was getting short, and over the next few days, Mercy and I grew closer and closer. Now that her terrible secret was off her shoulders, so to speak, we were able to talk more objectively about our respective experiences and feelings about what had happened to us and how we ended up in such awful marriages. Mercy began to feel lighter within me, and I was glad I had helped ease her burden. I began to know her as the woman she would have been if not for Hugh Tylden. What a clever sense of humor she had! She also had a vast knowledge of many things I knew nothing about, and there was now clarity about who she was and why we were meant to find each other.

And then there was Richard. I hadn't forgotten about him, and all modesty aside, he hadn't forgotten about me either. I told him that I was doing research for a book I was writing, and that I needed the few quiet hours each day at the café for that purpose. Afterwards, he would walk out with me, and we would stroll around Trafalgar Square, or sit on a bench and watch children feeding the hundreds of pigeons that flock there. I felt that I was being sensible and safe—it was daytime, there were always people around us, and he never suggested

going anywhere at night by ourselves. Though if he had—I
might have said yes. It seemed that he wanted to take things
as slowly as I did, and that was a refreshing experience. I
really didn't think anything would come of it, what with my
having to leave in a couple of days, but who knew what might
be possible?

I spent as much time with Mercy as I could. We truly
became sisters in spirit, if not in blood, and some remarkable
things took place in the days that followed.

I asked her once if she was able to come into and inhabit
my physical body.

"If you could," I said, "I'd take you out and show you
the London of today. You won't believe your eyes at how
large it has grown, and Mercy, you—we—have *got* to see the
Millennium Dome—"

"No, Lucy, I am not able to come into your whole body.
Nor am I allowed to leave this place at all. But there is
something—"

"What?"

"What I can do is let little parts of me enter you. Your
eyes, for instance, or—Lucy, if you would allow me, I—no,
this is too presumptuous of me to ask you."

"Ask me anything, Mercy. Please."

"Well—all right. But you may refuse, and I will
understand. Do you know, can you guess, what I have missed
more than anything since I died?"

"What's that?"

"Food. I have missed the pleasure of eating most of all. I
was quite a good cook, you know, despite what Hugh said, and
every Sunday, I made the most delicious steak and kidney
pudding for dinner. It was my mother's receipt, and it was a
famous one. I could not get enough of it. I think I could have
lived on nothing but that. So, if you would be so good as to . . ."

My brow furrowed a little. I could see what was coming.

"Lucy, you would do me the greatest of favours if today
you would order the steak and kidney pudding that they make

here. Perhaps even have two? My mouth could enter yours, and I could feast upon what I have not tasted in hundreds of years. It would be like a piece of heaven for me."

"Well, Mercy, it's—I'm—well, I've been a strict vegetarian for years and years. I'm not sure if—"

"It would not actually be you eating it, my friend, it would be me. Do you understand? Oh, Lucy, I would *so* love some. Just this one time, dear, I beg of you."

How could I refuse a plea like that?

The English language has no words to describe what it felt like when Mercy's mouth "took over" mine. Suddenly the teeth I'd had all my life were gone. My tongue was not my own. Mercy's teeth were a bit larger than mine, and sadly, some were missing, no doubt thanks to Hugh. But to have someone else's teeth in my mouth—well, as I say, there are no words for that sensation.

Then before I knew it, there it was in front of me, a very large steak and kidney pudding, and my hand was reaching eagerly for my fork. I had not eaten meat for probably twenty years, and here was an enormous forkful coming at me. I closed my eyes and opened wide, expecting the worst. My lips closed over it and—it was very odd, I could feel my jaws moving, my—sorry, Mercy's—teeth chewing and my throat swallowing, but I, Lucy, tasted nothing. Nothing at all. I had been afraid I might not be able to keep it down, but it was no problem.

When "we" had eaten every last morsel (and dismissed the idea of licking the plate), Mercy thanked me over and over, and said that was enough to get her through the rest of eternity.

(Side note: though it was Mercy's mouth that ate the steak and kidney pudding, it was my stomach that had to digest it later that evening. Luckily, there was an all-night Boots' the Chemist near my hotel. It wasn't a pretty sight that night.)

The next thing Mercy wanted to do was to come into my hands and fingers, so that she could touch my face and hair. I took out a compact and hairbrush for "camouflage." She had the gentlest touch of anyone I'd ever known, with the exception of my grandmother. She ran her fingers lightly over my forehead, down the ridge of my nose, around my ears, stopping at my earrings.

"They feel lovely, Lucy," she said. "I had always wanted to have my ears bored, but Hugh would not allow it. He said a curate's wife could not go round looking like a common trollop."

My hair was her next surprise, as I wear mine quite short. "How much easier it must be to care for it that way. By the time I died, my hair reached nearly to my waist, and it was a struggle to keep it looking tidy."

Then I felt her touch again, caressing my face so softly that it was like the wind blowing gently on it.

"Thank you, Lucy. I already knew you had a lovely face, and now I have touched it, you are even more beautiful to me now."

She was nearly overwhelmed when she took over my hearing. Even in a crypt that has become a café, there is a constant noise of dishes and silverware clashing together, workers in the kitchen calling out to each other, and tour groups shuffling in and out.

"But I love it, Lucy, in spite of the cacophony. It is the sound of living, breathing people, it is the sound of life itself. I find it most exhilarating. I almost feel alive again myself."

When I offered her my sense of smell, that too was something of a shock to her. We sat very still, sifting through the myriad of aromas. Food, sweat, dust, cleaning products, the very coolness of the crypt—she took all of it in, detecting everything that was in the air. It made me realize how little aware I was of odors in my world.

"Oh," she said, "I can smell that they are making steak and kidney pudding again today! No, do not worry, dear Lucy, I shall not ask you to do that again for me. Once was enough forever—for both of us."

Just about the only sense left she hadn't tried was sight. We decided to save that for tomorrow, the last full day I would have in London.

On my way out, Richard was waiting for me as usual, and I let him walk me back to my hotel. He asked how my book was coming along, and I told him I was quite near to the end of it. He asked if he would see me tomorrow, and I said of course. With that, he picked up my hand and kissed it as if he were a courtier and I a fine lady—what manners that man had!

*   *   *

It had come too soon. My last day with Mercy. With Richard. My flight was to depart early the next day, so this would be a sad goodbye to both of them.

I got to the café just as it was opening. When I sat down, Mercy and I exchanged our usual affectionate greetings. I sensed a heaviness, a sadness, between us—the knowledge that we would not be seeing each other every day. But neither of us wanted to speak of that yet.

I tried to sound happier than I was really feeling, and I know Mercy was doing the same thing.

"Today's the day that my eyes will become yours, Mercy," I said. "What would you like to see first?"

I was expecting anything but the answer she gave.

"What I should like, dear friend, is to see my own crypt, the place where I have lain for so many years. I have never seen it, you know, from the outside."

"Of course, of course, no, you could never have seen it. How stupid of me not to consider that."

"Never call yourself stupid, Lucy, for you know you are not. And neither am I."

"You're right, I take it back. After you have looked at it, should you like me to try and find Hugh's crypt? It may give you some satisfaction, some comfort to know you are safe from him forever. And I'll tell you what, Mercy," I laughed, "I'll be glad to spit on his grave for you if you like!"

"No, Lucy. You see, I already know which is his crypt. He died a few years before I did."

"Oh—I didn't know that. I just assumed that the many years of abuse and misery you suffered had caused your death."

"No," she said. "No, he died first."

"What—what happened to him? If you don't mind my asking."

She hesitated a moment.

"He died from head injuries he suffered in a fall. A *very* severe fall."

Mercy and I fell silent within each other. But in that silence, there was a sudden explosion of epiphany and illumination.

"Yes," she repeated. "He took a very bad fall indeed. Sadly, there was no saving him. I know I need not say any more about it than that. I am sure you understand."

In my mind's eye, I saw myself staring deeply into Mercy's eyes. She unflinchingly looked back into mine, and I was the first to blink.

Good for you, I thought. *Good for you.*

When Mercy entered my eyes, I forgot about my contact lenses. They immediately popped out, luckily landing on the table.

I stood up, with Mercy's eyes in my head, and moved away the table and chairs from above her crypt. The writing was faint and much worn, but I knelt down and we read:

MERCY CAROLINE TYLDEN
BELOVED WIFE OF HUGH TYLDEN
APRIL 4 1775-NOV 15 1823

"PEACE, PERFECT PEACE"

Mercy was the first to speak.

"Only now can I truly say that at long last, I have that perfect peace, the peace which passeth all understanding. All thanks to you, Lucy. Now I have but one final request to make of you, my friend. I know that your other "friend" is here, too—nay, do not blush, dear. I would very much like to have a glimpse of the one who has found favour in your heart. I want to see if he is worthy of you."

I slowly turned until Richard, at his usual table, was in view. He looked up and waved.

"There he is, Mercy. That is Richard. But I really don't think anything will ever come of our acquaintance, since I leave tomorrow. Though I must admit, it's been very flattering—"

Mercy's shriek was like a gunshot inside my brain. I collapsed in the chair, in real physical pain.

"Mercy, my God, what is it? Why did you scream? What's wrong?"

Her cries gradually diminished, and she gasped out, "He is—he is sitting over Hugh's grave. Over his *grave*, Lucy! Is that where he always sits? Tell me quickly, is it?"

"Yes, but—"

As we continued to watch Richard, he smiled at me. But this time, his smile was—it was so like—at last, I had remembered. Now I knew why he had looked so familiar. My former abuser had worn a smile exactly like that. And that smile never varied, whether he was battering me with his fists or with his words.

"Lucy, you must not, you *cannot* have anything to do with this person! He is not sitting where he is by accident. His smile is exactly like Hugh's, and I am terrified for your safety. You must tell him to go away. To leave us alone. *You have to do this, Lucy, it means life or death.* Oh, dear God, he is coming over here!"

And indeed, he was, with his hand outstretched to me. He looked down on me—us—with that self-assured—yes, and arrogant smile. Why hadn't I noticed that before?

Mercy's eyes were still mine, but I used my own voice and words.

I stood up. His hand was still out, but I did not take it. His confused look was gratifying, but I wasn't done yet. "Leave us alone," I said in a low but strong tone. "Get away from us this instant, or I will call the manager and tell him you have been harassing us. *Go away!* Shall I say this any louder? I can scream, you know. GO AWAY, AND LEAVE US ALONE FOREVER!"

I took a step forward as if to push him, and he backed up. Shook his head at me. Called me crazy. (And I think I was a little, just then.) But before he turned to leave, he stared hard into our eyes and said, "Oh, it's you, is it?" Then he stomped off toward the exit. I believe I heard him call me the B-word on his way out, and Mercy and I accepted that as a compliment.

*   *   *

Richard was gone, gone forever, we hoped. I was still shaking as I realized what Mercy had saved me from, but I also felt very powerful after ordering him to go away. Was it possible he was the reincarnation of Hugh Tylden? Or had he absorbed Hugh's evil by sitting where he did? I would never know, I suppose, but that was all right. I could live with the possibilities.

After Mercy and I had grown calmer, she was the first to say it.

"I know this day will be our last one together, Lucy. I am very sorry indeed, and will miss the comfort of our friendship."

"Yes," I said. "But I will come back, Mercy, if not next year, then the one after that. Our friendship will continue, don't worry about that."

"No, my dear friend. You have been such a source of strength and solace and love to me—and what you just did a few minutes ago in both our names—I will never forget. But we will not be permitted to be together within our spirits again. You and I were meant to find each other for a little while, and now we have found out why. There are no accidents in life. I think I will be able to sleep now, Lucy. Sleep like the innocent I used to be before my troubles. And though we may not be together in this way anymore, I know we will *always* be in each other's hearts. We are sisters forever, Lucy."

I wanted to cry out, *No, don't leave, stay with me, Mercy!*— but I did not. I knew she was right. She deserved to rest now, and I would not seek to interfere with that, even in the name of love.

"I won't forget you either, Mercy. I will treasure our time together forever."

"I want to give you a gift now, dear Lucy. I remember when you said you were sad because you had never felt your grandmother's spirit come to you, as your father's had done. This is my gift to you. I have gone abroad into the place of shadows where ones such as I dwell, and I have learned this: you never felt her spirit come, Lucy, because she has *always* been near you. From the moment she departed your world, she has never left your side, dear friend. She is with you now, and will be evermore."

I couldn't speak for the tears running down my face. Mercy had given me the greatest gift I could ever have. She had given me more, infinitely more, than mere possibilities, and I would never doubt or feel lonely again.

"Mercy, I don't have the words to say all that I feel. You know better than anyone what is in my heart now. I love you! Thank you for giving me back my grandmother."

I struggled on in spite of the tears.

"So we won't say goodbye, but farewell, dear Mercy. Sleep well. We *will* meet again, I am certain of it, when the time comes for me to shrug off this earthly body. We will meet again in your world."

"I am certain of it too, Lucy. Farewell to you until then."

I felt her spirit fade away. I sat until I knew she was no longer there, and then I bent over and pressed a kiss onto the top of her crypt. I rose and walked to the entrance of the café, where I paused a moment, thinking about something my grandmother had told me once when we were talking about heaven. She believed that each departing soul was like a ship that sets sail out of its harbor. We, the living, remain behind, watching the ship for as long as we can, but finally it gets so far away that it disappears over our horizon. But just at the moment when we lose sight of it completely, someone on the other side is catching a glimpse of it coming over *their* horizon.

As I stood at the door, behind me was a world of eternal shadows and never-ending sleep. Ahead of me was my future. I took a deep breath and stepped out into the sunlight.

Anything was possible.

THE LIGHT AT THE END

Let your light shine. Shine within you so that it can shine on someone else. Let your light shine.

Oprah Winfrey
O Magazine, January 2004

I love this dear old house. I was brought up here, and though I have lived in several different places during my life, I always end up coming back here. Coming back home.

I'm sitting in the front room, watching a glorious sunset through the picture window. She will be here anytime now, I know. I'm meeting my grandmother here. Though we've been separated for a while, we manage to speak every day without fail. We've both been looking forward to this reunion, and I'm already beginning to watch for her arrival.

She raised me when my parents died in a car accident. I was two at the time and don't remember them at all. I only know them through photographs and the stories my grandmother used to tell about them. My grandmother was everything to me—father, mother, sister. She *was* my family, and the beginning and end of her was absolute, unconditional love. There was never a time when she wasn't there for me. And I have loved her back in the same way, though I may not have always told her so. But I will tell her tonight. Tell her how grateful I am for her unselfish, loyal love. I'll make her understand what she has meant to me, and how her life has shaped mine.

She was born Mary Lucile Pence. She never cared for her first name. Anyone could be a Mary, she'd say with a twinkle in her soft, gray eyes, but there are not many Lucile's out there. The name Lucile means light, and I liked that, because she was truly the light in my life. As a child, I called her Cile. The name stuck, and that's what I call her today.

Now the sun is beginning to go down, and the room is darkening, but I won't have the lamp on just yet. It's very pleasant to sit here in the shadows, quietly waiting. It's easy to let my mind drift off, and scenes from my life with Cile play out in front of me like an old home movie. The years fall away and I am a child again.

I am five and we are sitting together in the porch swing. It is high summer. My head is in her lap, and I drift in and out of sleep as she sings "In the Good Old Summertime." She strokes my hair so tenderly, so gently, and I feel safe and strong in her love. The rhythmic squeak of the porch swing, the shrill sounds of cicadas and crickets, the cozy smell of warm gingerbread, and my grandmother's touch. Life was simple and good, and I was a happy child with Cile loving me.

Cile taught me to read before I ever started school. She would read aloud to me and with me every night at bedtime, sometimes from my favorite book of fairy tales, sometimes from the books she was reading. I came to know P.G. Wodehouse and Jane Austen as well as I knew Cinderella and Peter Pan. I have no doubt that her reading to me instilled in me a love of words and of the books that contained those words. And nor do I doubt that she inspired me to become what I am today, a writer. A minor one, to be sure, though I was never minor in her eyes. In fact, what I am writing now is my tribute, my final homage to the woman who loved me into the person I've come to be.

(Now I hear her, she is here! But no, it's only a tree branch scraping the side of the house. Never mind, I will be patient.)

And now I am seven, starting school, and having a very difficult time. I was different, having no parents or siblings. I was the odd one, the last to be picked for a team, the girl that others stared at without wishing to know me better. Up until that time, I had not been around children who were my age, only my grandmother, and consequently I felt closer to my teachers. I was a good student, but I was teased, sometimes unmercifully, because Cile was obviously so much older than my classmates' parents. I was often late going home because I had been crying, and I didn't want Cile to know. It would have hurt her feelings dreadfully to know, and I believed it was easier for me to just accept the taunting and insults of the other students. I don't know what would have happened to me if things had gone on in this way, but somehow—and to this day, I still don't know how—Cile found out how I was being treated. Perhaps the teachers told her. But she did find out, and then she set about, in her own subtle way, to help me make some friends. She began paying calls on my schoolmates' parents, taking me with her, bringing me forward, and talking about me, my background, my accomplishments, my interests, and so on. She forced me to speak up, to talk about myself, thus helping me to break through my shyness, and that allowed my classmates and their parents to realize that I was someone worth getting to know. It still brings tears to my eyes to recall what she said at every house we visited. "Come here, darling," she'd say with a loving, encouraging look, holding my hand firmly in hers. "I want to introduce you to some very nice people."

In time, her scheme worked, and I began to make some friends. Not very many—I've never been the type to have a large circle of friends—but enough to make me feel "normal," more involved, and less isolated. Cile was always asking my friends over to our house for sledding parties with hot cocoa afterwards, sleepovers on the weekends, or just to play. Board games, charades, amateur theatricals—there was rarely a dull moment in our home. She had a carpenter build a tree house in our back yard that was the envy of the neighborhood. She passed on to me her old dollhouse, and my girlfriends and I spent hours with it, rearranging the tiny furnishings, and making up stories about the family who lived in it.

It was good to have friends, but I think it was perhaps even better for me to have gone through the first difficult times too. I learned to be comfortable and contented not only with being by myself, but with others as well. I was sometimes *alone*, but I was never *lonely* after that. And that's how it's been for the rest of my life. Once again, Cile had stepped in, and changed the course of my life for the better.

(I get up and look out the window. It is full dark now, and I watch for her, still not seeing her, and feeling a little anxious. But I know—I know—she will be here soon. She promised me.)

I am fourteen now, lumbering through adolescence, worrying equally about acne and my periods, final exams and what college to choose. I developed countless crushes that I never spoke of, but thought about and sobbed over at night after I'd gone to bed. I was not one of the "popular" girls, not a cheerleader, or even a band member. My strong suit was writing and foreign languages.

Then, at long last, one of my crushes actually asked me out, my very first date! He was to pick me up at 7:00 PM for dinner and a movie afterwards. Cile was almost as excited as I was, and she helped me pick out a becoming outfit and took me to have my hair done. I thought Saturday would never arrive, but at last it did, and I began to get ready at least two hours ahead of time. I treated myself to a long soak in a scented bubble bath. I dressed myself with care, and took countless nervous looks in the mirror from every possible angle. Finally I presented myself to my grandmother, and the love and pride in her face showed me better than any mirror could, that I could not be more beautiful. We sat down in the front room to wait at 6:45. Cile saw my shaking hands, and told me everything would go just fine. "Just be yourself, darling," she said, "and that boy won't know what hit him." I smiled wanly and tried to take courage from her. 7:00 arrived. 7:15. I picked up a book and pretended to read. Then it was 7:30. Cile picked up a book and pretended to read. When it turned 7:45, I finally had to broach the awful idea—had I been stood up? "No," Cile said. "No, we'll just give him a little more time." Then, after the boy was more than an hour late, Cile and I just looked at each other, and we both had to accept the traumatic fact that I had indeed been stood up. I tried but failed to hold back my tears and humiliation. Cile at once became an angry mother bear protecting her cub. It was just as well the boy never showed up, because he would have been blistered beyond recognition with her opinion of his behavior. He was unworthy, unreliable, and showed a shocking breach of manners, she said, and she wouldn't have wanted me to be with someone that rude and inconsiderate anyway. She comforted me as only she could. A few moments of heavy silence, she snapped her fingers and said, "I know! Let's go downtown and spoil ourselves with ice cream!" And we did—she ordered a root beer ice cream soda, and I indulged in a banana split. Before long, we were talking and laughing so much that I nearly forgot that I had been deserted and ill-used by my crush. Today I don't remember the boy's name, or even his face, but I will always recall how Cile got me through my first heartache.

(I look at my watch, though it's too dark to read the time; but I know it won't be long now. I can feel it, I feel her, coming to me.)

How homesick I was my first year at college! It was the first time I'd been away from Cile, our home, our town. Now I was among strange faces, trying to understand confusing class schedules, navigating my way (and usually getting lost) around a huge campus, and I knew I would never, ever fit in. After two weeks, I called Cile in desperation. "Please, please, please let me come home. I am *miserable* here! Please, Cile, bring me home!"

She told me no. Years later, Cile said that was the hardest thing she ever had to do. It broke her heart to say it. She asked me to hold on a little bit longer, that things truly would get better, and to just give it more time. For her sake. As I hung up, I thought I would never stop crying. I felt abandoned by the only person who had ever loved me. I ran back to my dorm room and locked it. Threw myself on the bed. I thought the pillow would muffle my sobs, but in a few minutes, there was a knock on the door. It was the girl from the next room down. Could she come in for a while and visit? She didn't seem to notice my tear-streaked cheeks and swollen eyes. She sat down and told me about her first year here, how out of place she had felt, how she had almost dropped out. She was so glad she hadn't, because she eventually made some friends, and that, she said, had made all the difference in the world. And would I, by any chance, like to go out for pizza that night with her and her roommate?

That was my last sad time in college. And I bless Cile in my heart daily for having been strong and courageous enough to say no to me at such a crucial time in my life.

(I must finish this soon. It's almost time.)

And so I lived the rest of my life the best I could, according to the principles Cile had instilled in me. Actually, it was just one principle—love. Simple, unconditional love.

I persevered in my writing career, with small successes here and there. I loved and married a man who loved me back and would never have considered standing me up at any time. We had lovely children, who in turn had children of their own, and Cile became a great-grandmother. I tried to be to all of them what Cile had been to me, and whether I accomplished this or not, only time will tell.

My husband died twelve years ago, and our children are all grown and scattered and have families of their own.

Cile has been dead for nearly twenty years. Now it is time for her to keep her promise to me, and I ready myself. I've truly had a good life.

I lie down on the couch and stare out into the darkness. I think I hear—yes, I do hear music from far away—"In the Good Old Summertime"—then the touch of gentle hands in my hair and on my face, and soft fingers closing my eyes. Closing them forever on this world, and opening them in the next. But I am not alone. *She* is here to take me, to lead me with her loving hand in death as she did in life. She will bring me home at last. I feel her very soul closing around me, easing my hurts, quelling my fears, and loving me. Loving me. Just loving me.

"Darling," she says, "I want to introduce you to some very nice people."

"I want you to meet your parents."

I go joyfully into that welcoming.

And it's a very great light indeed.

REUNION

They say that blood is thicker than water.
Maybe that's why we battle our own with more energy
and gusto than we would ever expend on strangers.

David Assael, *Northern Exposure*

It was meant to be a good house. A happy house. It's not, now. But it could be again. If I can only do what needs to be done for this sad house—this house of hate and prejudice and fear. It has frightened me for too long; it has divided the closest of families. It has even killed. Good versus evil? I don't know. I don't use those words lightly. Everything in me says that evil does not exist, that "evil" is simply our own misperceived separation from God. And since nothing can ever separate us from God, there can be no real evil. But this house—I am forced to believe that there *is* something there, some malevolent presence, sick with enmity and corruption, poisoned with cruelty and bad blood. I know it's there because I have felt it, felt it call to me, beckon to me. And once, it almost took me. I know this house and I think I know how to heal it. If it can happen at all, it will happen tonight. I think this will be a very long night.

I have lived in this house for a long time now. My parents, knowing but not completely believing its sordid history, bought it for a good price at a public auction, and we—my parents, my older brother Will and I—moved in after six months of major renovations. We have lived in Gideon all our lives, and we'd heard all the wild and improbable stories about our house. And the stories went back, it was said, to long before my father, and his father before him, were born. Back to when there was no house at all, only a battlefield where a Civil War skirmish took place in 1863.

Before war came to it, the land had been all gently rolling hills, sunny meadows, and thickly wooded forest. Afterwards, the hills, meadows and forest still stood, but the ground was sodden and befouled with the blood of men, some of whom perhaps never fully understood why it was that they were to kill each other. Sixty years later, the state took it over and turned it into a tourist attraction. The Battle of Gideon Hill, they called it. And today, not many people who live here can tell you with any certainty who actually won the battle. All that remains of that bloody fight are two gravesites, set at opposite ends of the battlefield. Both mark the resting place of an unknown soldier, one from the North and the other from the South. I used to wonder about those graves—who the men were, what had become of their parents, wives and children, and whether anyone today ever thought that once upon a time, those men had been tiny, helpless babes, with pure, innocent souls that knew nothing of guns and war and bloodshed. Every year, a contingent of Civil War re-enactors came to lay wreaths on the graves, but did anyone truly care about the two who, through no fault of their own, lay beneath that field?

As a very young child, I can recall my grandfather telling me stories about the strange things that sometimes happened on the battlefield grounds at night. Whenever there was a full moon, the battlefield was an irresistible attraction for boys who wanted to play soldier or cowboys and Indians. There were hills to crawl up and surprise attack the enemy; trees to lurk behind for ambushes; and the graves—they were where vanquished foes were carried and dumped unceremoniously onto the ground. But every now and then, according to my grandfather, there would be a night when a boy, no matter how brave he thought he was, ran home as fast as he could, to breathlessly relate a tale of hearing low moans and cries and sometimes of even seeing a ghostly form, dressed in blue or gray. This had happened once to my grandfather, and he swore to his dying day that he had really heard and seen those unearthly things. I was too young to differentiate between truth and a tall tale, so I asked my father once whether he had ever had a similar experience. He said no, he hadn't, that I shouldn't believe everything I heard, and that he would prefer that I not be in the battlefield at night anyway.

About forty years ago, some part of the land directly across from the battlefield went up for sale. Gideon's mayor bought it, and he built a large, handsome, three-story house for him and his family. Though it was a private home, it gradually came to be called "The Battlefield House" by residents of the town.

And thus its ghastly life began.

By the time we owned it in the early 1980's, there had been probably six or seven families who had lived there. Lived there for a time, then abruptly sold it. Or just abandoned it, deserting it in the darkness of night, hoping they were leaving the house and the bad dreams it caused, far behind them.

I don't pretend to recall exactly what strange events happened to which families, or when. Some of the things that I do know, I have heard from the townspeople or the homeowners themselves; others, I know because I was there.

The first casualty was the mayor's family, about three years after they had built their house.

He had had a bad habit of smoking big, black cigars. And unluckily for him, he smoked them at night, in bed. It was assumed afterwards that the fire began in the bedroom. The house was not completely destroyed—just the bedroom. When the flames were finally extinguished, the firemen found the mayor and his wife still in bed, sleeping the sleep of asphyxiation. They probably never knew what was happening. They were the lucky ones.

After the house was restored and sold by the mayor's heirs, what the local newspaper described as "unfortunate events" began taking place from time to time. For the next thirty years, every family who lived there suffered in some terrible way.

The first set of people to live in the house after the mayor were always fighting water coming into the basement every time it rained. And it seemed to rain an awful lot in the two or three years that they were there. After a while, all the trapped moisture drifted upstairs and mildewed their clothing, curtains and furniture. The people were determined to stay, so they reinforced the foundation, had their clothing and furnishings steam cleaned, and thought their problems were over. Wrong. After a day of shopping, they came home one day to find that nearly all the wallpaper had peeled away from the walls and was lying on the floor like large wood shavings. They tried to convince themselves that that was due to the mildew, too, but within a few weeks, a For Sale sign showed up on their front lawn.

A young couple came to look at the house and fell in love with it. It was no time at all before the papers were signed and a moving van was parked in the driveway. They had hopes of starting a family there very soon. But the house had other ideas. Poor things, it was just one miscarriage after another for them. And when the wife finally did carry a child to full-term, he was born with birth defects so severe that they had to institutionalize him almost immediately. The nursing home where they placed him was over fifty miles away, so it wasn't long before they, too, sold out and moved to be closer to their child.

It was right after they left that people began to talk about The Battlefield House. Neighbors on either side of the house spoke of hearing strange noises and seeing odd things—they never would elaborate, as if afraid that those things might be visited upon them if they told. Some people started calling it The Bad Luck House. Others, more literary, called it The Boo Radley House. Over time, kids stopped playing in the battlefield opposite. If they had to pass the house, they ran or went another way. It was as though the house had been taken over by—here's that word again—some form of evil.

The next family to own the house was sleeping peacefully in their beds one night when a tiny piece of a meteor punched its way into their roof with a mighty crash. It narrowly missed their twins' bedroom, but it did hit the dog. He did not die, but bore a long bare gash along one of his back legs for the rest of his life.

One of the creepier things that happened to the same owners was the invasion of the frogs one night. They kept hearing something scratching around all the outside doors, and when they looked out, there was a veritable sea of frogs all very intent on coming in. They finally had to get the garden hose out to wash them back. In the morning, the frogs were all gone—it was as if they had never been there at all.

Another set of owners woke up one morning to find long scratches all up and down the lengths of their two cars—which had been in the locked garage all night. The repairs were covered by their insurance, but they were dumbfounded at how such a thing could have happened. Then a few weeks later, they discovered minute cracks in all their windows, which they had to replace. They chalked that one up to shifting tectonic plates beneath the earth. At least that's what they told the neighbors. They lived in the house the longest all of the owners (with the exception of me), but the final straw came when the electrical system went haywire. They'd turn on the lamp and the garage door would open. Switch on the television and the food processor would begin whirring away. That was enough for them. Another For Sale sign was staked out front.

I'm only giving the highlights of the horrors, so to speak— I don't have enough time to detail all the other things: the divorces; the wife who sometimes had to shield her black eye from the neighbors when she went out to get the mail; the couple who awoke one morning to find their bed infested with cockroaches; the child who broke a leg falling from a tree house that a former owner had built; the only son who never came back from Vietnam; the son who did return safely from Vietnam, only to be killed by a drunk driver on the way from the bus station to his house; the baby who was accidentally scalded in the bath when the tepid water suddenly turned boiling hot; the pets who appeared to cower or growl at nothing when they were outside; the flower beds that were flourishing one day and wilted and dead the next. Little things and big things. Taken separately over thirty years, they added up to—well, maybe just plain old bad luck. But taken all together, it was more than obvious that there was something or someone in that house that was unhappy. Very unhappy indeed.

The last of the owners (before we bought the house), a feisty lady of at least seventy years, had known there was something very wrong with it. That's why it took six months of renovation before we could move in. The neighbors reported a disturbance one afternoon, and when the police got there, they found the old lady energetically swinging away at the house with a sledgehammer. She had broken through most of the walls and windows, and was just starting in on the doors when the officers stopped her. She was wildly insane by then, of course. As the ambulance took her away, she was heard to shriek repeatedly, "The dreams! The dark! The dreams! The dark!"

So that's where we came in. As I said earlier, my parents got a good price on it when it was auctioned off. They were pretty down-to-earth people—they knew all the stories and the bad reputation of the house—and yet they chose to buy it and move us into it. I'm not sure whether they just did not believe in the stories at all or whether they were simply too stubborn to let a so-called "bad luck" house keep them from doing what they wanted. Either way, it didn't matter. Because the house ended up working us over, too.

We had lived in the house for about a week, when my brother Will, two years older than I, first noticed something was wrong. He was upstairs one morning getting ready for school. I was in the kitchen eating breakfast with my parents. Suddenly we heard Will galloping downstairs, taking the steps at least three at a time. He skidded into the kitchen with a handkerchief over his nose.

"Jeez," he said. "What's going on with the furnace?"

My father asked him what he meant.

"Can't you smell it? It's just like—it's like that dead woodchuck we found in the ditch the other day."

We sniffed around downstairs and couldn't detect anything. Then we accompanied Will up to his room, and sure enough, there was a stench like rotting meat pouring through his register. I ran to my room in alarm, but everything in there was normal. And after checking every other room in the house, it appeared that the smell was only in Will's room.

It had permeated everything in there, and Mom eventually had to have the whole room fumigated.

"Probably just a dead mouse in the vent," said my father. "I'll take a look at it when I get home tonight."

"But if it's in the vent, wouldn't *all* the registers—?" My mother never finished her question, not after she saw the look on Dad's face.

And so our troubles began.

*   *   *

In the beginning, it was rarely anything big and dramatic like some of the previous owners had experienced. The incidents were sometimes a nuisance, like when Dad's car got a flat tire every day for four days. (Roofing nails, Dad said.) Then there were more serious ones. One morning, we came downstairs for breakfast, and as soon as we entered the dining room, we all—*all four of us*—got bloody noses at the same time. We laughed and called it an odd coincidence, but I think it was because no one wanted to admit that we were getting a little more frightened each and every day.

And there were much scarier things to come.

It was a few weeks after we had moved in. We had pretty much unpacked everything, but there was still one more box left. Dad opened it and stuck his hand in, then suddenly let out a cry of pain. He drew out a bleeding hand and stared at it dumbly for a moment. Mother rushed him over to the sink and started running cold water over the wound. While she did that, Will looked inside the box.

"Wow!" he said. "Whoever packed that box is in big trouble."

I hesitantly peered over the edge. Cutting edges all facing up, a layer of variously arranged kitchen knives, scissors, and electric saw blades filled the bottom of the box. It was as if they were waiting for the right person to come along for them to bite.

"Well, it sure wasn't me," I replied. "And Mom wouldn't have packed things like that anyway. Only an idiot would do something like that, or somebody that *wanted* to . . ." My words trailed away into silence, as my brother and I stared at each other.

"Do you think—I mean, first there was that smell in my room, and that time we all got bloody noses. I don't know about you, but I've been having some really freaky dreams—do you think all the things we've heard about the house are true? That it's really haunted? Or whatever?"

"I don't know," I said. "But we'd all better look twice before we do any more unpacking. And—so you've been having strange dreams? Funny, I have, too."

"What were they like?"

"Oh, I can't really describe them," I replied. "I've usually forgotten them by the time I'm good and awake. They're not too bad. Just dreams."

Mom had just finished bandaging Dad's lacerated hand, and they came back into the room. Dad looked like he wanted to say something, but he only tightened his lips. He looked in the box again, and that was the first time I ever saw my father afraid.

It was also one of the few times I'd ever not told my brother the complete truth. I *had* been having the most awful dreams—or actually, only one dream, the exact same one, night after night. That dream would always leave me gasping and drenched and weak when I awoke from it. And I remembered every terrifying detail.

In the dream, I'm walking through the dining room, and just as I go past the stairs leading to the second floor, I stop. Or something makes me stop. I don't know which it is. Anyway, I stop at the bottom of the stairs and look up into the dark. And it's a dark that's blacker than dark, somehow. I'm looking into the darkness and I become aware that there is something up there that wants me. Wants me to come up and make its acquaintance. And I know that whatever it is, it is the most evil thing that I could ever imagine. It is overpowering my strength and making me move unwillingly toward the steps. *Wake up, wake up!* I keep screaming at myself. And just as I reach for the railing and put my foot on the bottom step, I wake up.

I wanted to tell my family about the dream I was having, but every time I would start to, something in me would tell me not to. I don't know if it was my inner voice guiding me or what, but I just had a strong feeling that it would be best for me and for all of us not to speak of it. To handle it myself. It was frightening to go through, but I kept telling myself that it was only a dream. Not real. And "not real" couldn't hurt me. Besides, I always woke up in time before anything bad could happen. So I said nothing. Now I understand that my not telling was exactly the right thing to do. It will help me with what I need to do tonight—what I must do to purge and restore this sad, bad luck house and let it become what it was always meant to be, a healing and comforting shelter. A home, not just a house.

The next person to get hurt by the house was our mother. Will and I got home from school one day to find her resting on the chaise longue in the sun porch. Her forearm was a solid swath of white. She had broken her wrist earlier that day.

She didn't remember much about it. She had been taking some clean towels and sheets upstairs, when she missed a step and started to fall forward. She couldn't seem to stop falling *up* the stairs. "It was the funniest thing," she said, trying to laugh, but not quite making it. She kept trying to catch herself by grabbing at the railing and the walls, but she just kept on falling upwards. "I must have made one hell of a racket!" When she finally regained her balance and could stand up, she felt a stab of pain—that was her wrist. She called a neighbor, who took her to the emergency room.

"Just me being clumsy," she cheerfully explained when Dad got home. Again, she tried to pass it off as a joke, but nobody was laughing. After dinner, I overheard her telling Dad that when it happened, she could have sworn she felt like someone was pushing her from behind. Nope, not funny. Not funny at all.

Over the next two years, things continued to happen. To go wrong. The washing machine spinning out of control and ending up on the opposite side of the laundry room; the four of us coming home from a school event and finding every door and window standing wide open; opening the morning newspaper and a dead rat falling onto the breakfast table. These things were creepy and startling, but at least the house seemed not to want to actually injure us anymore.

Then our world fell apart in one evening.

Will was getting ready to graduate from high school. During his teenage years, he and Dad had butted heads on more than one occasion, but their minor disagreements had always blown over. Dad and Will were really quite close because their personalities were so much alike. Sadly, that would also prove to be their undoing. One night at dinner, Will announced that he would not be going to college in the fall, though he had easily passed all his entrance exams and had a full scholarship. My parents were shocked, to say the least. But that was nothing compared to how they reacted when they heard what his plans were: to enlist in the Army and serve his country.

"Will," pleaded Dad, "You can't do this, son. You *have* to go to college. You can't expect to get anywhere without a college degree. You—you've always been so good in math and science. I just assumed you were going to major—"

Will broke in.

"Mom, Dad, I've done a lot of thinking, and I really believe this is what I need to do. I know you're disappointed and everything, but I'm just not ready for school. I can learn about computers and math in the Army. It's my decision and my life. I have to do this. I'm sorry."

Dad and Will went back and forth for half an hour, with Mom putting in her two cents whenever there was a break in the discussion. But it was no good. Will was determined to enlist, and nothing that Dad could say would make him change his mind. Dad didn't lose his temper very often, but he did now.

"Goddammit, Will, you've got to listen to reason! You may be eighteen, but you're still a child and you don't know anything about life. You're throwing your future away with both hands. Please, son, why don't we drop it for now, and talk about it later on this summer? Then, if you change your mind, your scholarship will still be there."

Will set his jaw.

"It won't work, Dad."

Dad set his jaw, too.

"And why not, may I ask?"

"Because I've already signed the enlistment papers, that's why. I report to Fort McGie for basic training two weeks from today."

Mom turned pale and Dad went beet red.

"You what?" he yelled. "You actually went behind our backs and—how could you do such a thing? Did you even *think* of your mother, of me, of your sister? Christ, that's the most immature, irresponsible thing I've ever heard of. I—I can't even begin to make you understand what you've done. But if you want to be stupid and not listen to—oh, hell, just leave the table, Will. I don't want to discuss it any further right now. Go upstairs to your room, and you'd better do some hard, fast thinking while you're there."

"No."

"Excuse me? Didn't you hear what I told you to do?"

"Yes, I did, Dad, and I'm not doing it. I'm eighteen and old enough to decide what I will and will not do. And I will not take orders like that from you like I'm some kind of—of puppet!"

And with that, Will jumped up from his chair, knocking over a water glass. Mom and I looked at each other, scared to death. She reached and took my hand in hers under the table. Dad was standing up, too, and father and son glared across the table at each other for what seemed like eternity. It was Dad who broke the silence. His voice was cold and distant.

"Fine, then, you just go ahead and do what you want. You won't listen to me? Well, that's great. I guess you'll have to learn the hard way. And since you think you're so grown-up and mature, you can start your new life by leaving this house. Now. Tonight. Go upstairs and pack your things. I don't want to see you again. Do you understand me?"

"Yes sir, I sure do. Well, don't worry, you won't see me again. I'm sorry, Mother. I'm sure it's better this way."

Will ran upstairs and soon we could hear closet doors and drawers opening and slamming shut. I couldn't believe he was really leaving, and I couldn't believe Dad was letting him. Ten minutes later, he came into the room, suitcase and backpack filled to bursting. He bent over Mom, who was still in shock, and kissed her cheek. Then he ruffled my hair and said, "See ya, kiddo." He paused briefly by Dad and stuck out his hand, a hand that trembled slightly, as a peace offering. Dad refused to take it. He wouldn't even look at him. Will straightened up and walked stiffly out of the room, out the front door, and out of our lives.

*   *   *

It's hard to make myself realize that so much time has passed since that terrible scene at the dining room table. I'm now on the downhill side of thirty, and yet it seems as though it happened only last week.

Dad and Will never spoke again. Will stayed at a friend's house until he left for boot camp. He didn't call us before he left. He never wrote afterwards either. It broke Mom's heart, yet I know he didn't do it deliberately to hurt her. I think he probably felt that if he were to communicate with any of us, he might break down. He was stubborn, my big brother. He got it from his father.

By common, silent consent, we never talked about Will. The years came and went. He simply vanished from our conversation, though I know we all thought and worried about him—even Dad, though his pride would not let him show it. No, it was as if Will had never been born.

Mom took his leaving the hardest, I think. She had a woman's heart, a mother's heart, and unexpectedly, that heart ceased to beat one afternoon while I was away at college. Dad called to tell me the dreadful news. He was nearly hysterical. He had come home from work and found her lying at the base of the stairs in the dining room. An autopsy was done, and it was determined that it had been a severe and sudden stroke. The doctor told us she almost certainly never knew what was happening. No pain, no awareness, she just slipped away into death as easily as one would slide into a warm bath. Dad and I tried to be glad that it had been that way for her, but it was hard, very hard, not to have been able to say goodbye to her. Not to hold her hand and tell her how much we loved her. Everything felt unfinished and incomplete, for weeks, even months, after the funeral, because we had not had those last moments with her. I desperately wanted to let Will know about our mother's death, but I had no idea where or how to reach him. And there was something else, too, something I know my father and I were both thinking, but dared not bring up: *Had the house taken her?* We never spoke of it, ever. The idea, once brought forward, would have driven both of us mad.

Dad naturally did not want to live in the house alone, so I took some time away from school and helped him find and move into an efficiency apartment in town. We talked about putting the house up for sale, but we never took the necessary steps. So the house sat alone and empty, with only its own ghoulish, infernal presence to keep it company.

*   *   *

After I received my degree in journalism, I came back to Gideon to be near Dad. I got a job as junior copywriter for Gideon's newspaper, which was fulfilling and interesting. Dad's small apartment wouldn't hold both of us, so I decided to move back into the house. After all, we still owned it. I asked my father many times to come back there with me, but his answer was always the same: he would never set one foot in the house where his wife had died. I felt just the opposite. I *wanted* to be in the place where she had made a home for us for so many years. It made me feel closer to her. It was where, once upon a time, before all our troubles, we had been a solid, united family.

It took me several weeks to make the house livable again. I took the dustsheets off the furniture, washed curtains, vacuumed and dusted, and got the utilities turned back on. After I had things arranged to my liking, I deliberately walked over to the base of the stairs. The stairs where Mom had been found dead. I stood there a moment lost in thought. I remembered Mom and Will with tender love and a longing to go back to better times. I suddenly realized I was becoming angry, wildly angry at the entity in that house that had caused my family—and all the families before us—such misery. I glared into the darkness at the top of the stairs and called out to—I didn't know what.

"Hello? I don't expect you to answer me, but I know you're there. And I want you to know that I'm not going to be afraid of you anymore. You can do anything you like, but you won't drive me away. Do you understand? I won't take it anymore. Your time is over. You got that? Your time is over!"

While I was in college, I had stopped having the dream about the house. But on the very night I was once again under its roof, the dream came back, and I started having it every night. And like before, I'd wake up just in time, right before I started up those steps. Any hopes I'd had that the house's malevolence might have waned in the years it had stood empty were gone.

Dad and I gradually fell into a regular routine. He would never visit me at the house, but I would pick him up several times a week, and we would go out to dinner, take a drive in the country, or see a movie. He seemed to be satisfied with his solitary existence, but I could see through the façade. He was older and grayer, certainly. But there was also something in him that seemed like it was being starved, little by little. Grief was taking him away. He grieved not only for his dead wife, but also for his only son, who might also be dead, for all he knew. A son he had once loved, and still loved, deeply. There was a yawning emptiness in him that could only be filled and nourished by Will, his long-lost son and my brother. It hurt me to see Dad fading away, and I was determined not to let him leave me, too.

And so last night, as I was working on the computer, I suddenly decided to write about and describe in detail my recurring dream. When I got to the place where I always awoke, a startling idea came to me. The more I thought it about it, the better I liked it. It felt right to do, and I believed that my inner voice was guiding me again.

What if I didn't *let myself wake up from the dream in time?*

Could I make myself mount those steps into the darkness and confront the unknown? It seemed so obvious that the answer I sought was waiting up there to be discovered and brought into the light. And I was the only one who could do it. I prayed I could do it.

So tonight is the night of final reckoning. For the sake of my mother, Will, and Dad, I will bring this house home. I must try, no matter what.

*   *   *

I'm lying on the sofa downstairs, waiting for sleep to overtake me. As I drift off, I mentally order myself to not resist the dream. I want to dream, I must dream, and I will not let myself wake up until I have climbed those stairs and learned the black and haunted secret of this house. My family's soul depends on it, and I must not fail. Don't wake up. Don't wake up. Don't wake—

It's no good, I can't get to sleep. I sit up and look at the clock. It's just past midnight. Maybe some warm milk will help me relax. I get up and head for the kitchen, passing through the dining room.

I freeze just as I get to the bottom of the stairs. I feel it again. There's something there, something up there at the top that wants me. It wants me so badly that I can feel its hunger, its eagerness, its readiness. I don't want to go, because I know it's evil. I won't go, but I watch in horror as I helplessly approach the steps. I'm not sure if I'm awake or asleep. I look up, expecting to see it, but it's making me to come to it. Moaning a little, I reach for the railing and put a tentative foot on the first step. There. That's all. I can turn around now and go back to bed. But no—I am forced to keep climbing toward the bad darkness, and slowly but relentlessly, it calls me, leads me, pulls me in. I am weak, I cannot fight it, and I can hardly breathe for how frightened I am. Is that my heart booming like that or is it thunder? No, it's not my heart or thunder. It's like—like gunfire, only deeper. And then I recognize the sound. It's a cannon. I finally reach the landing at the top of the stairs, and I see a smoky, foggy mist that swirls and dances just in front of me. That mist surrounds me now, and I strike at it, as if at a mosquito. I can't see anything. Can't hear or feel. But I can smell an acrid burning like gunpowder. I stand still inside the mist and I know that when the air clears, I will see the foul face of evil that will not let this house rest.

The fog slowly begins to dissipate, and I turn in a slow circle until I think I see something. There is a form there, yes, I do see it now, it's shrouded in blackness as I knew it would be and I can feel it staring back at me. Strangely, all fear leaves me as the figure gradually becomes visible. It's *not* a dark, malevolent monster, ready to devour me.

It's a lady.

A lady dressed in the deepest mourning, with a translucent black veil covering her face. Her dress is not of this time. It's full and voluminous, and reaches all the way to the floor. She wears a jet brooch at her breast. It has a woven design with two different shades of hair inside of it. It's difficult to guess the lady's age, but she looks very fragile and she seems to tremble all over. I can just barely make out her features through her veil, and I see that her face is indeed that of old age. It is lined and careworn. It is a face of unbelievable grief and loss. Tears run down her cheeks, though she makes no sound. Not fearing anything now, I reach my hand out to her, to offer comfort and sympathy. I can feel the sadness of her soul reaching back to me.

"You are so unhappy," I say. "Can I—can I do anything to help you?"

She speaks as if from a great distance.

"Yes, child. Excuse my calling you that, but I feel as if you were my child."

"Are you the—the spirit that haunts this house?"

"I am."

Relief, anger, disbelief, and pity wash over me as I ask her, "Why have you done such awful things, why have you made all those who lived here so unhappy all these years?"

"I have been here a very long time, child, and I had no other way to communicate with the living. *You* are the first person to possess the courage and strength to come and seek me out."

"Then what do you want of me?"

She takes a black lace handkerchief from inside her sleeve and gently wipes the tears from her face.

"My story is similar to yours, my dear. My family was torn away from me, and I ache to be with them again. You can help me by reuniting us."

I suddenly remember my mother and how she died and I am immediately angry.

"Why should I help you, when you took away my dear mother?"

I turn on my heel and begin to walk back to the stairs.

"Wait, my dear, please don't leave," she cries, "*I* did not cause your mother's death. It truly was a stroke that she died of, and it would have happened whether I had been here or not. You must believe me. I would not do such a thing to you."

She sounds like she is telling the truth, and I don't know why, but I feel as though I can trust her.

"All right, then. I will help you, if I can. Where is your family, and how am I to do what you ask?"

"It is a sad story, my dear, but I know you are the only one who will understand it. My beloved husband and our darling only child, our son Seth, lie not far from here. When war came to our country, our son, a mere boy of seventeen years, wanted to go and fight with the others. We told him we would never allow that. He was our only child, the pride of our lives, and we knew he would likely be killed were he to become a soldier. He and my husband nearly came to blows one evening over it. The next morning, Seth was gone. He had run away to join the fighting, you see, and we could not trace him. In desperation, my husband went off to find him. After several weeks, he finally discovered him in a field where there had been a recent fierce battle. Seth lay dead of an opposing soldier's bullet. While my husband was trying to lift him to carry him away, the battle began to rage once more. My poor husband suffered a mortal blow from cannon fire, and fell to the ground with his arms around our beloved son. And when the smoke and noise of war were all gone, their bodies were discovered. I want to join them, child. That is the only way I can have peace at last, and that is why I called you to me."

As I listen to her story, tears roll down my face. My family did know the same loss she had suffered.

"Where will I find—" I begin to ask, but I suddenly realize I know the answer.

"Yes, child, you have guessed rightly. They are buried in the two gravesites in the battlefield just over the way."

"May I ask—did your son fight for the North or the South?"

She bows her head, places a shaking hand over her brooch and says through tears, "Does that really matter anymore, my dear?"

And she is right—it doesn't.

"I will gladly do anything I can to reunite you with your family. Just tell me how."

I listen closely as she tells me.

*   *   *

Time passes. Minutes? Hours? Days? Time has no meaning anymore. I slowly awake and find myself lying on the dining room floor. There is an afghan covering me. I sit up, confused and disoriented. I must have been walking in my sleep, something I've never done in my life. I examine myself to make sure I haven't fallen or hurt myself in some way. I stare at my hands, my clothing—they're absolutely filthy. Dirt is caked under my fingernails. I have a blister starting on one palm. As I try to clear my head, I catch sight of a metallic object next to me on the floor. A garden trowel from our shed. What in heaven's name did I do last night? "Heaven"—the word triggers a vague memory of something. I think I went outside to help someone who was in trouble. I'm starting to remember now. Yes, my dream. I didn't let myself wake up. The grieving lady of this house and her lost family. She asked me to do something for her and I did it. It's like looking through the wrong end of a telescope, but I see myself walking across the road to the battlefield and digging up soil from both graves. I put the dirt in a bag, and shake it all together so that it is united—no, *re*united. I return to the house and take the bag upstairs. I offer it to the sad lady in black, and she smiles and cries and takes the bag and holds it close to her breast. And I know whose hair is woven together in her brooch. Now that she once again has all that is, and ever was, dear to her, everything in front of me—the lady, the bag, the sounds of cannon fire and grief—they all simply fade away. The house seems to heave a great sigh as they go, and the very air around me feels lighter. I'm tired and dazed, so I go downstairs. I don't even make it as far as the sofa. I just lie down on the floor, and as I'm falling asleep, I feel a trembling hand place the afghan over me, and that same hand caresses my hair softly for a moment, as if to thank me. Then it is gone. Gone forever. And I am happy that the "unknown" soldiers are unknown no more.

* * *

I had to spend extra time in the shower later that morning, just to get my nails clean. I had finished toweling off and had put on my bathrobe, when the doorbell rang. I peeked through the steamed up bathroom window and could just make out that it was Dad. He was actually here at our house! I ran to the door and opened it. And couldn't speak for shock. Standing in front of me with their arms around each other's shoulders were Dad—and Will.

"He just—he just showed up at the apartment this morning," Dad said hoarsely, and tried to say more but couldn't speak through his tears. Then we were all crying and laughing and hugging and trying to recover the lost time, the lost years.

And I learned a lesson.

Nothing—and no one—stays lost forever. Someone always finds them and brings them back to where they need to be.

It was a joyous reunion for all of us.

THE MALL WALKERS

To be alone is to be different, to be different is to be alone.

Suzanne Gordon
Lonely in America

It's just after 9:00 A.M. and I am once again sitting on a bench in this shopping mall, a bench that I've come to consider my own. Any minute now—yes, I can hear them coming, hear them long before I see them. All the various people who work in all the various stores here. Some stroll, others hurry as if late, but only one thing stands out to me—they all know each other—at least that's how it looks to me. They laugh and joke among themselves, and as they walk past me on my bench, I pretend for a moment, as I always do, that I am one of them, on my way to work, to my own job. But they pass me by every day, looking through me, around me, over me, but never, ever at me. Yet I have the feeling that without seeing me, they know all about me. How I'm in between temp work and abusive boyfriends. No longer on the medication that's become too expensive for me to buy. The shabby, dark room that I am several months behind on in rent. How as I get sadder, I get smaller, and that as I get smaller, I get sadder. That I'm like the lone goose that's lost its life mate, and is consigned forever to be alone, to be different, always the odd one in any group. Whenever I see a flock of geese passing over, I compulsively count them. If it's an even number, I know they're all happily paired up, and that makes me feel better.

I know I need to be out looking for work, but it's easy to just sit here and drift. To wish I were a child again, with parents to look after me and take care of my needs. I know I'm falling deeper and deeper into a hopeless trap, and these dark thoughts go round and round my brain in the same endless circle . . .

"Good morning, young lady!"

I jump, startled, and look around. It's a group of mall walkers, and they have stopped briefly by my bench in their track around the mall. I've become acquainted with the group, well enough to know that one of their fellow-walkers has passed away recently. I've counted them, too, and come up with an odd number. Very sad.

The lady that spoke now smiles at me, and asks how I'm doing. It's her eyes. Her eyes tell me that she sincerely wants to know. I thank her and say I'm doing better. It's what I always say. The other walkers all smile and nod at me and invite me to join them for a lap or two, but I decline and say maybe next time. They tell me to have a good day, then the group moves off, seemingly as one mindless, walking entity. One of them looks back at me, and winks encouragingly. Her purse strap slips off her shoulder, she catches it, and then the whole group disappears around the corner.

It's a small gesture, but a kind one, and it makes me feel for a moment that anything might be possible, that this might be the day I get a job, or make a friend. I let myself hope a little, just a little, and it's enough to get me off my bench and on my way to the exit to catch the bus downtown. Halfway to the door, though, I realize I've left my jacket on the bench, and I return for it. It's still there, undisturbed, and that's a relief, because it's the only coat I have. But there's something else there, too. A wallet, a lady's wallet lying right next to my jacket. Surely one of the mall walkers lost it, so I sit back down, resolved to wait for them to come around again so I can give it back.

But they never come back.

I wait and watch for them for nearly an hour, and almost decide to walk after them, to catch up to them. But then I'm suddenly aware of how tightly I'm clutching the wallet, and how warm and supple the leather feels in my hands. I'm aware of other things, too—visions of my paying the back-rent, buying food, medication, clothes—getting a respite from my never-ending worry and sadness. I'd always heard that money cannot buy happiness, but I'd be satisfied with just a few moments of feeling safe and secure.

I've done some not-very-nice things in my life, but until that moment, I had never stolen someone else's property. I believe I must have gone a little crazy at that point, because suddenly I'm standing completely outside of myself, watching me grab up my jacket and tuck the wallet into one of the inner pockets. And I run for the door, just in time to meet the bus. It was as though I'd rehearsed this scene for months. Every movement was smooth and flawless.

I don't dare to let myself think until I'm safely back in my room. I unlock the door, and the only sound breaking the silence is that of me turning the deadbolt once I'm inside.

*   *   *

. . . and back at the mall, the group returns to where the girl had been. She is gone, and so is the wallet. They share a silent, mutual delight, and renew their pace around the mall. Soon they will be complete and whole once more, and now there is something to walk for, again.

*   *   *

I don't know how long I sat on the floor with my back against the door, trying to quiet my racing heart. I think I might have fallen into a state of other-consciousness, because when I came back to myself, I was disoriented and groggy. I wasn't sure of the day, the time, or how I had ended up back here. Then the truth slowly began to seep into my brain. A memory of having been at the mall, sitting on my bench; then, yes, one of the mall walkers had spoken kindly to me; and then I remembered leaving the mall quite quickly, because . . . because . . .

It all burst in on me at once what I had done. I shut my eyes, hoping I'd awaken from this bad dream, but when I opened them, I could no longer deny it. I looked down, fearfully (but I have to confess, hopefully, too), and there, my hands holding onto it as if it were a lifesaver, was the wallet.

Oh, no, please God, I thought. *It's true, really true, I have done this horrible thing. Taken someone else's lifeblood and identity.* Had I truly fallen this far into the abyss? And having fallen, would I ever be able to get out again?

But there was another voice that spoke within me. A bad voice. One that said *too bad, so sad, finders keepers, losers weepers. One man's loss is another's gain. If you can't take care of your possessions, then you don't deserve to keep them.* And all I could think was that I had lost and wept for too long, too long.

I opened up the wallet. There was money in there and I eagerly pulled it out. It felt good in my hands. I counted the bills—fifty, one hundred, two—dear God, I was holding almost $500! Mine now, though. All mine, and no one could make me give it back. I threw the now-empty wallet aside, and it fell open to a picture ID of its rightful owner.

I picked the wallet up again and studied her photo for a long time. My feelings flew back and forth between guilt and joy and shame and relief. She was obviously on the wrong side of 70. *What was an old woman doing with so much cash— oh, of course, pension check. I must put that thought away right now.* She had snow-white hair, carefully permed, and her wrinkled face was dotted with liver spots. I looked closer. They weren't wrinkles exactly—they were more like lines that life had carved into her face.

It was a shock when I saw her eyes.

Those weren't the eyes of old age and loneliness and poverty. There was a timeless sparkle of youth and strength in them that I envied. Hers was a face that was at home and comfortable with itself. And though forty years must separate us, I'd have given a great deal to see the same innocence and serenity in my own eyes.

As I sat there holding the money in one hand, and the wallet in the other, ideas and images poured into my brain: the grandmother who had raised me after my folks separated, and who had died just last year; my dark, damp living quarters with the peeling wallpaper and tattered curtains; the ever-growing stack of unpaid bills on the kitchen table; an old lady frantically pawing through her purse, looking for a wallet that would never appear; and finally, a strange and eerie vision of an invisible fishing line attached to the wallet, that someone would pull away every time I tried to pick it up. As it kept pulling away from me, I wondered who—or what—was on the other end of the line?

When a child steals a piece of candy, his first impulse is to get rid of the evidence right away—he stuffs the candy into his mouth as quickly as possible. I was feeling the same thing. I must spend this money right away before they take it away from me. After all, I reasoned, the crime had been done and couldn't be undone. I would spend the money only on things that would help me better myself and my sad situation. And one day—I didn't know how or when—I would find a way to make it up to this woman who, in my disordered thoughts, I was coming to think of as my benefactor. Yes, someday when I was secure with steady work and money in the bank, I would take under my wing another friendless, down-on-her-luck girl like me, and become her mentor. *Her* benefactor.

My thoughts ranged further on. Anyone who looked as happy and contented as this woman, whose money I now was clutching, would probably not regard the loss as a total tragedy. She would have family and friends to help her—*I* did not. I was sure that if she could only know how much, how very much I needed this money, she would not begrudge me for a second. Not someone with such a kind face.

I mentally slapped myself. I was just making excuses, rationalizing the crime, bribing my conscience. It was no good. If I could not be honest in other things, let me at least be honest in this: I took the money because I needed it, and now I was going to use it to help myself.

I folded up the wallet and hid it under my bed pillow. I left my room with the money crammed in my purse, looking fixedly down at the ground as I walked to the bus stop, not daring to meet anyone's eyes. I had to fight an uncomfortably irrational fear that if anybody were to lock eyes with me at that moment, they might suck the very soul out of me.

*   *   *

I did not return to the same mall, of course. There was another one on the other side of town. In a few short hours, I emerged from it with almost more than I could carry. I felt I had spent wisely, not frivolously. I bought some basic but good outfits that I could wear to interviews and work, shoes, and a winter coat to replace the thin jacket I'd been making do with all year. I refilled my medication prescription for the first time in months. I stopped at the grocery store to re-stock a nearly empty larder. And I still had money left to pay a little towards the back-rent and utility bills. Next week, I planned to get the phone turned back on. They had cut off my service months ago. In spite of all the bags I was carrying, I was feeling lighter than I had for years. Maybe it would be all right after all.

When I returned home, I carefully and lovingly put away my new things. I became aware that I was feeling less different, and more like a normal person. Normal people had enough to wear and enough to eat. Normal people had jobs to go to, and I was certain I would too, perhaps even by the end of the next day. Normal people had friends, and I was still that lone, solitary goose, but again I trusted that when I got work, I'd get friends the same as anyone else.

That night I cleaned my room as I never had done before. I borrowed the landlady's vacuum and worked for hours, clearing away layers of cobwebs, scrubbing the floor on my hands and knees, putting fresh sheets on the bed. Everything smelled fine and good and clean when I was done. I felt the same way inside, too. I also cooked a real meal for myself, nothing fancy, but for the first time in months, I could really taste the food. I went to bed tired, but it was a good tired.

Before I turned out the light, I got the wallet out from under my pillow and looked at the woman's face again. I mentally thanked her and hoped she did not hate me for what I had done today. I pretended for a moment that she was my grandmother, and I humbly kissed her picture, asking her forgiveness and suppressing a sob.

I dreamed the strangest things all night long. In one, I was chasing after some people, convinced they had stolen something from me. I would almost catch up to them, then they would simply speed up and disappear around a corner. In another, I was looking at my reflection in a mirror, and I suddenly realized it was *not* me, but someone else. But the most vivid one was where I had taken hold of the wallet, and a hidden trap sprang, catching my hand in a painful, vicious grip that I could not release. I was just beginning to gnaw through my wrist, when I awoke with a stifled scream.

I did manage to get some sleep in spite of the dreams, and when the alarm went off the next morning, I flew out of bed, actually looking forward to the day ahead of me. I had it all planned out. First thing, I would update and make copies of my resume, go to the temp agency and get job leads, then fill out and leave applications for work at each place. I felt confident that I would end up with a job that very day—or the next, at the latest. Then with some regular money coming in, I would eventually paint my room, dark and tiny though it was, put up some bright new curtains, and maybe buy some inexpensive pieces of furniture. It was funny, I mused. Yesterday I'd been jobless and only a few steps away from being homeless. Now I was ready to make things happen for me, and I felt something I had not felt for a very long time— I felt in control of my life. Most people take that for granted in their lives, but it was truly a rare and precious gift to me.

Breakfast, a long, hot shower, my hair styled becomingly, and wearing one of the dresses I'd bought the day before— I looked in the mirror, and unlike the dream of the previous night, I saw my real self looking back, looking attractive and professional. I left my apartment with my head and hopes high.

The day was an utter disaster.

First, I had made several odd mistakes on my resume— I'd put 1945 instead of 1995, stupid little things like that. So I re-did it, checked it carefully, and made enough copies to see me through a dozen interviews. But dealing with those mistakes made me arrive at the temp agency later than I had intended. Being late made me nervous, and my stomach was beginning to hurt a little. By the time I got there, a lot of the better job leads had already been given out, but I sat uncomfortably in the job counselor's office while she came up with a few more for me. I stood up to leave, and saw to my horror that I had started my period—that was the stomach ache, I guess—and had not only soaked through my new dress, but the chair pad as well. I apologized again and again, but the counselor said not to worry, it could happen to anyone. After I got out of the office, I wanted to cry, but I pulled myself together and went home to change clothes.

By the time I was ready—again—to leave, I was really running behind. I was positive the bus would be slow in coming, but it wasn't, and I began to feel a little better. Maybe I could still salvage something out of this day. But my bad luck held. When I arrived at the first place, an insurance office, I had no sooner begun to fill out the application than my pen ran out of ink. I got another from my purse and as soon as I touched it to the paper, it leaked and made a huge blotch on the page. I had to ask for another application as well as a pen, and I could see by the look on the personnel manager's face that I was not making the impression I'd hoped I would.

When I finally completed the form and handed it in, I was thanked and told that they would let me know. I knew all too well what *that* meant, and I went on to the next place, an accountant's office, feeling off-balance and flustered.

Things went wrong there, too, the worst of which was that I actually misspelled my own name. *What was wrong with me today?* I was practically speechless with embarrassment. Also, I had to make an emergency stop in the restroom—I was having an abnormally heavy period, it seemed. Great, just what I needed.

Halfway into the next interview, I swallowed the wrong way and couldn't stop coughing. The more I tried to stop, the worse it got. They finally sent someone to bring me a glass of water, which I immediately spilled on the table. I don't remember how the rest of the interview went— thankfully—but I left knowing that I had not gotten that job either.

I had one more place to go, but I just couldn't put myself through any more that day. I was so shaken and confused that I got on the wrong bus, and it took me twice as long to get home.

I cannot adequately describe how shocked and demoralized I was at how the day had gone. But it was nothing compared to what I felt when I opened the door of my room. As I stood there looking in, I saw complete devastation. My first thought was that I had been vandalized, but as I looked closer, I knew no person could have done this. The place looked like it had not been touched in decades. It looked dead. I *knew* I'd spent hours cleaning the night before—I had not dreamed that. But now there was a thick layer of dust coating everything. Cobwebs hung from the ceiling as if I'd been decorating for Halloween. There was a palpable haze of dust in the air.

I took a few tentative steps inside. The floor, which I'd washed and waxed on my hands and knees not twenty-four hours before, was unspeakably sticky. So sticky that when I took a step on it, one of my shoes came right off my foot. When I bent down to pick it up, I saw, to my revulsion, that there were countless flies, ants, and cockroaches glued to the floor. I didn't know which was more disgusting, the ones that were already dead, or the ones that were still struggling to free themselves. I was in such a state of numbness by now that seeing bodies of dead mice, scattered here and there, barely registered.

My sleeping area was no better. The fresh sheets I'd put down were fresh no longer, and I saw right away that I would have to throw them out. There was not enough laundry detergent in the world to clean them. Dirty laundry lay sprawled and stuck hopelessly to the floor. Mouse droppings covered the tops of my tables and dresser.

Then it got worse.

I slowly was becoming aware of an overpowering stench coming from the kitchen. I crossed the floor on tiptoes, dodging insects and vermin, and opened the refrigerator door. The smell rushed out at me and hit me like a fist. All the food I'd bought the day before was rotted and rancid. Sour, curdled milk, putrefied vegetables, gangrenous-looking hamburger, and, worst of all, mold—mold growing everywhere, even up the sides of the appliance and spilling out onto the floor. I barely made it to the sink in time to throw up. I didn't think I would ever stop, but I finally had nothing left in me.

I got a newspaper and spread it out so I could sit down in the chair. I kept looking at the filth and squalor around me, asking myself how this could have happened. I went through every emotion a person could feel—rage, grief, wonder, despair, disbelief—everything except—

The phone began to ring.

I had not gotten the phone turned back on yet.

And that's when I finally began to feel afraid.

It rang and rang and rang. Whoever it was, was persistent. Finally I picked it up.

"H-hello?"

"Hi! I was just checking to make sure we're still set for tomorrow."

"I'm sorry—I don't know who this is. How did you get this num—?"

"We'll plan on seeing you in the morning, the usual time, bright and early, ok? Have a great evening!"

"But, wait—I—who—"

The caller had hung up.

I retrieved a blanket that wasn't too filthy and wrapped it around me. I sat in that reeking room, trying to make sense of something that had no sense to it at all. Who had called me? And *how* had they called, since the phone had been disconnected for so long? Was it someone from one of the companies I'd interviewed with that day, offering me a job? But I couldn't convince myself of that, reasoning that they'd given no name or mentioned anything about a job. Just that they'd see me tomorrow. See me tomorrow—those words went round and round in my brain. I couldn't stop them. They just kept on going. It was like my thoughts were—were the mall walkers, traveling in an endless circle, forever and ever, without end.

Mall walkers. The wallet.

That's it, I thought. *That's why this is happening. I took what was not mine, and now I am being punished for it.*

Now things at last began to fall into place.

But who or what was doing the punishing was something I could not let myself think about.

At least now I knew what to do. I had a plan, and I would carry it out, first thing in the morning. I'd make everything all right, then *I* would be all right, too.

It was a long time before I dozed off, but I was already feeling a tiny bit better.

* * *

I didn't sleep too well that night, curled up tightly in the chair. I awoke stiff and sore. But after splashing some cold water on my face and drinking a cup of lukewarm instant coffee, I felt more clear-headed. I didn't bother to change clothes—the dress I'd slept in was wrinkled, but I had more important things to think about.

The first thing I did was get the wallet out and put it in my purse. Next, I collected the things I had bought the day before, along with the receipts, and put them back in their original bags. The food and the stained dress, of course, I couldn't return. I got to the mall just as it opened, and I was glad when the salesperson did not protest my request for a cash refund.

As I put the money back in the wallet, my soul felt lighter. I knew I was doing the right thing, the only thing, to ease my conscience, though I realized it would never make all my guilt go away. But I was satisfied, and almost excited, about the next and final thing I had to do.

I took the bus to the other mall and immediately headed for my bench. I nonchalantly glanced around, making sure no one would see as I slipped the wallet from my purse and placed it on the bench. What a sensation of relief I felt then! And if I am to be completely honest, I must say that the relief was mixed with loss, too. I was back to being alone and jobless again, with no secure future in front of me. But at least I didn't have the stolen wallet to worry about anymore.

I didn't see any of the mall walkers yet, but I was certain they'd be passing by soon. And then I could go home and make an effort to clean up the horrible mess in the room I'd left behind.

I turned and began to hurry towards the exit, much as I had done when I'd first taken the wallet.

A hand fell on my shoulder.

Gasping, I whirled around.

They were all standing there looking at me, those nine mall walkers. After a long silence, one of the men stepped forward.

"Excuse me, miss, but I believe this is yours," he said.

He was holding the wallet out to me. I felt the blood drain from my face and I thought I was going to faint.

"No, no—it's not mine," I stammered. "I was just returning it. I didn't mean to—it's just that . . ." I ran out of words and breath at the same time.

"No, I'm *certain* this is yours," the man said and chuckled a little. The others smiled and nodded in agreement. They came a little closer to me, and suddenly I understood. They had meant for me to have the money! They had seen that I needed help, and had purposely left the wallet for me to find. Such dear, generous people!

Now one of the women took the wallet and tucked it into my purse, then patted my arm. I was wondering how I would ever be able to thank them enough, and was getting ready to say so, when I noticed that they had formed a sort of semicircle around me. They said nothing, only looked at me. I was a little uncomfortable, and began to back up. They matched me step for step until eventually they had surrounded me. I was in the center of the group, and no matter where I turned, there was no place to go. Something was very wrong, and I was very frightened. *Who were these people?* As I blindly spun around looking for escape, my purse strap came loose. It was gently placed back on my shoulder, and with that touch, I seemed to fall away from myself, fading and falling, falling and fading, until . . .

. . . round and round the mall, we continue our endless circle. I lag behind for a moment, catching sight of my reflection in a store window. But it's not me. This person has hair the color of snow, and what I first take to be freckles, are old age spots. Then I look deeply into her eyes and see youth and strength and peace that seem to defy the heavy lines and wrinkles of her face. She looks familiar somehow, and I smile at her, only to see the exact same smile given back to me. My (our) eyes widen, and I (we) suddenly understand. As I hurry to catch up with the group, I reflect that I am no longer the lone, odd goose. I am mated for life now. And that makes us an even number at long last.

THE GAME

All paid jobs absorb and degrade the mind.

Aristotle

For Randy

I work in a gift shop in a large shopping mall. Though our store is small, our stock is eclectic: we carry everything from jigsaw puzzles to silver teapots. We employ anywhere from four to eight people, depending on the time of year, and we've all gotten to be pretty good friends. Our boss is Mr. Schultz, and I'm the assistant manager. There might be better paying jobs, but certainly none that are less stressful than this one. I've been here now for—let's see—I guess it's been five-going-on-six years. But I may be retiring soon.

Recently, one of our employees quit. Didn't give us any notice whatsoever. She was the last person I'd have expected to do something like that, and I guess I feel kind of responsible because I had been in charge of the store right before she quit.

This happened in January. That's a really slow time for us. Our stock is depleted from Christmas and customers seem to be all shopped-out. Business doesn't start picking up again until May, in time for Mother's Day and graduations. It's lucky we employees all get along so well, since we end up doing a lot of standing around in the winter. Sometimes a whole morning goes by without a customer. Time hangs heavy, and you can only do so much shelf cleaning, silver polishing, and display rearranging.

Our boss's mother had died the first part of the year and he took several weeks off to go out of town and clear up her estate. I was left in charge of the store. I wasn't anticipating any problems, and I think we all felt a little relieved about Mr. Schultz being away. Less restricted. He's a nice guy to work for, but he tends to hold himself a bit aloof from the rest of us. But that's part of being the boss, I suppose.

For the first couple of days, I went slightly overboard in my zeal to "run" the store. I had the two daytime employees dusting shelves, putting up new displays, and cleaning jewelry until even I couldn't ignore their grumblings. So I loosened up a little. They were good workers, very pleasant to have around. Richard had worked there almost as long as I had, and Freda—she's the one who quit—had been there about two years.

Richard, Freda and I were fairly close in age. Freda was the type who would say little about herself, but was always ready to listen to your problems. She still lived at home with her parents, and was desperate to save up enough money so that she could get a place of her own. She was a kind and gentle person who had a practical outlook on things. And as for Richard—well, he had what you would call an outgoing personality. He always had a tall tale to spin and would swear it was true. Listening to him pacify a dissatisfied customer was a real object lesson in Dale Carnegie. He was about the most intelligent person I'd ever met, and that intimidated me a little until I got to know him better. There was no meanness in him, but he did get some pretty strange ideas and notions every now and then.

It was Richard who introduced us to a silly game he'd thought up about a week after the boss left. He called it the "What-Would-You-Do-For-a-Million-Tax-Free-Dollars" Game.

I think the reason it got started was that we just ran out of things to talk about one day. We'd already discussed our favorite movies, our worst blind dates, and what we'd had for dinner the night before. We were bored, and Richard didn't like bored. One afternoon, we had been grousing about our personal finances, or lack thereof. Freda especially was sensitive about this, because, as I mentioned, she was trying to get her own apartment. During a lull in the conversation, Richard suddenly got a faraway look on his face and asked us, "Say, what would you guys be willing to do for, oh, let's say, a million tax-free dollars?"

"Oh, just about anything," I joked, and we all laughed. "What did you have in mind—you know—before I actually commit myself?"

"Well, let me think a minute." He looked up at the ceiling. "Ok, I got one. Would you parachute off the water tower?"

"And just who is going to give him this million dollars?" Freda asked him a little sarcastically. She sometimes got impatient with what she called Richard's "flights of fantasy". "It's all about the What-Would-You-Do," he replied. "Not so much the Who. Although I *do* know a man—" Richard stopped and tried to look mysterious. And failed, as usual. He never could keep a straight face.

"Ok, I see what you're doing," I said. "It's one of those games about what three books would you take with you to a desert island, or if there was a fire, what would you save first, a baby, a priceless painting, or your grandmother."

"Yeah, right. Something like that."

Freda got intrigued in spite of herself, but true to form, took a practical view. How high was the water tower? she asked. Could you take skydiving lessons first? Would your hospital bills be deducted from the million dollars?

Her questions soon got us going. We all tried to come up with unusual, if not downright ludicrous, situations. Would you swim the English Channel in a hurricane? Live in the woods for three months with only a book of matches, a Boy Scout knife, and your wits? Rappel down the Grand Canyon? Go over Niagara Falls in a Glad trash bag?

And so our game—no, **The Game**—was born. It began innocently enough. It challenged our creativity and it never got old, because we were always coming up with new ideas, new situations. And within a week it had become our main source of conversation. Freda said she found herself thinking about it at home, driving to work, and before going to sleep at night. I started writing down some of the better ones we came up with. Richard was very pleased, I could see, that he'd gotten us so immersed in his fantasy.

In fact, we got so involved that our ideas gradually started to get a little crazier, a little more over-the-top. Like: for a million tax-free dollars, would you eat only banana yogurt for one month? Not bathe or shower for two months? Shave your head and get a dragon tattooed on top of your bare skull?

Carry a Tickle Me Elmo doll around with you everywhere
and talk to it? Never again cut your toenails?

And of course there was a catch to all this: you could not
tell anyone why you were doing these things, or you would
forfeit the million dollars.

Freda was the one who introduced the disgusting food
motif: would we, she asked, eat a pound of uncooked snails
at one sitting? Raw liver? Slugs? An entire can of Crisco? A
brimming bowl of pond scum? Whenever she came up with a
new idea, she'd get the giggles so that we could hardly
understand her, and that made Richard and me crack up too.

It was odd that, levelheaded as Freda was, she was the
most reckless one of us. For that kind of money, she claimed
she'd do nearly all the things we thought up. Not even the
snails put her off. As for me—well, I knew it was just a game
(small "*g*"), but actually, there weren't many things I would
really have been willing to put myself through. No, I wouldn't
have walked naked through our mall at high noon on a
Saturday, or waved like a maniac at every car I saw like I
knew them, or ordered chocolate pudding in a restaurant and
eaten it without using fingers or utensils. Not me. I was too
chicken (or too self-conscious) to even consider these things,
though I laughed just as hard at them as the others did.

And then—I don't remember exactly how or when it
happened—**The Game** started to go weird on us. It got mean
and bad. Like it was playing us instead of the other way around.

And that's when I started feeling a little uneasy. A little
not right.

At some point, we all realized we had somehow stopped
playing it just for fun and laughs. We began going for the most
disgusting, horrifying and—yes, wicked—things we could think
of. Going for the gross-out, as we used to say. And we had added
another rule: once you said you'd be willing to do something,
you'd have to stick to it. No changing your mind later.

Now we were coming up with some really awful stuff.
Would you sit at the bottom of an outhouse during a 24-hour

chili and beer party? (Freda asked if you could have an umbrella.) Would you drink a pitcher's worth of the combined spit of all the employees at the mall? Let someone throw up on your hair and not wash it for two weeks? Drink an entire bottle of castor oil and not change your underwear for a week? We were not only addicted to **The Game**, but had become almost frantic to outdo the others in ideas. We couldn't *not* play. But at that point, we didn't want to—and maybe couldn't—stop ourselves. I should have done something. I was the assistant manager, but I was as hooked as the rest. I really should have done something.

On and on we went, darker and deeper. Would you sleep in the same bed with a dead person? Take a dog from the animal shelter, skin it alive, and wear the fur around your neck? Feed rat poison to your sister's baby? Eat a dead woodchuck? Tear off all your fingernails with your teeth? Have all your teeth pulled without anesthetic and never get dentures?

Oh, yeah, we were addicted.

But the absolute worst was to come. It was a Friday, and the boss was due to come back on Monday, so we were trying to straighten up the store a little. Richard called us over to the jewelry counter. I could tell by the look on his face that he had gotten what he called "a juicy one." I almost told him not to say it, for all of us to just shut up and go back to our real work, and stop playing this stupid mind game. But I didn't, and oh God, how I wish I had.

Freda and I stood there, waiting for Richard to speak.

"Ok, ok, I've got one. The best one yet. You guys ready?"

He ran his tongue over his lips and said, "For a million tax-free dollars . . ." He paused for effect. "Would you bite off all of your fingers on one hand and eat them?" Then he burst into high-pitched and uncontrolled laughter, slapping his knees and bending over.

I bent over too, but it was because my stomach had turned over and I thought I was going to be sick. The mental image was just a little too vivid. That's when I knew I'd had enough.

But Freda, practical to the end, asked, "Can you get prostheses put on afterwards? Do you have to swallow the fingers whole, or can you cook them first? Do you have to keep them down? And would that include the thumb, too?"

"Ok, Richard," I said, "That's the worst one yet. Hooray, you win. Now why don't we all go back to doing what we get paid to do?"

"Yeah, but would you do it?" Richard persisted. It was like he *had* to know our answer.

I looked at him for a long time, trying to read his expression. "No way, man," I finally said. I walked back to the aisle I had been arranging, shaking my head. I was done. Done and disgusted with the others, **The Game**, and myself.

But Freda continued her questions: Could you pick which fingers? Did you have to go all the way to the back knuckles? Would you get more money if you broke a tooth while gnawing through the bones? And would the money be given in cash or check?

Richard and Freda laughed and talked a little more, then they eventually quieted down and started working again. We didn't really have another chance to talk until closing time, as several customers came in at that point and kept us busy for a while.

I'd been getting a really unpleasant feeling all afternoon, and it only got worse as the rest of the day passed. I felt like I'd hurt someone I loved or done something illegal. A kind of soiled feeling. What had started out as an amusing way to pass the time had degenerated into a horrid kind of sordidness. Again, I felt like we were no longer in control, that **The Game** had taken over. But at least I'd taken a stand for myself, though perhaps too late, against playing it anymore. This may sound really funny for a guy to say, but I felt violated, like my mind had been raped. I had "been around the block" a little, but it was as though something that was still innocent and good in me had vanished. I didn't feel good. Not one bit.

That evening as the three of us walked to our cars in the parking lot, Richard started in again.

"Hey, how about this one, guys, for a million tax-free—"
I stopped him. The guy just didn't know when to quit.
"Come on, Richard. We've done this to death, wouldn't
you say? What do you think, Freda? Aren't you tired of it, too?"
Freda nodded, but didn't say anything. And as I drove
away, I saw the two of them sitting in her car, talking.

*   *   *

That weekend, I worked my butt off cleaning my apartment
from top to bottom. I wiped off the top of the refrigerator,
dusted under furniture, and even waxed the floor under my
bed. I don't have an English Lit degree, but even I knew that
what I was doing was really symbolic. I was cleansing myself,
my mind—hell, even my soul—of the horrible mental images
we had been entertaining ourselves with. To my shock, I
actually found some banana yogurt in the fridge and couldn't
throw it out fast enough. When I saw a stray dog cross my
lawn, I cringed. And when my sister called to tell me my niece
had begun crawling for the first time, it was all I could do not
to slam the phone down. What had Richard—no, what had
The Game done to me? To the three of us?
It was a long and lousy weekend for me, and I was back
at work early on Monday. Mr. Schultz was already there,
checking figures and reports, and he and I walked around the
store, discussing minor changes in the merchandise displays.
Richard arrived ten minutes late, with his usual contrived
excuse. But Freda had still not shown up by the time we
opened the doors. It was unlike her not to at least call, so the
boss finally phoned her. After he hung up, he informed us
that she was not sick, but that she had requested she be
allowed to take her two-week vacation starting that day.
Richard had a strange look on his face when he heard this.
"I told her that wouldn't be a problem," Mr. Schultz said.
"We're slow right now, and we can call one of the part-timers
to fill in for her."

With the boss being back, Richard and I worked a whole lot harder than we had in the previous few weeks. I mean, we actually did our jobs. We still had time to talk—about the movies we'd seen, what the Royals' chances for the World Series were, and yes, we even fell back to describing what we'd had for dinner the night before. The game—thank God I had finally stopped thinking of it in capital letters—gradually faded away until it was only a nightmarish memory. Richard never brought it up again, and I was thankful for that. I kept meaning to call Freda and see how she was spending her time off, but for some reason never got around to it.

Two weeks went by, and we were all there the day Freda came back. Our jaws dropped as she walked in the store. She was *gorgeous*. She'd always dressed well and looked as attractive as her limited budget would allow, but now—she was wearing an expensive-looking dress, and it sure looked like silk to my untrained eyes. Over that, was what had to be a real fur coat. Brown leather gloves, new shoes, gold earrings, a strand of pearls and a new hairdo completed her ensemble. She looked wonderful, but there was a sort of pinched look around her eyes, as though she were tired or in pain. But how could anybody be tired after two weeks off?

She said she was glad to see us, but couldn't stop to chat. She had to talk to Mr. Schultz. She tapped very gingerly on his office door, entered, and shut the door. The sense that something was wrong grew in me as I listened to their muffled voices rise and fall. Freda's tone was calm, but I could tell that the boss was surprised by what she was saying.

Several minutes went by, then the door opened and they came out. Freda went to her locker and began gathering her things and putting them in a bag. Mr. Schultz stood nearby, looking puzzled. She spoke a few more words to him, then they shook hands. It seemed to me like Freda flinched a little. As she approached Richard and me, she was juggling her purse and the bag awkwardly from one hand to the other. She hugged Richard, whispered something to him, then turned to me.

She put one gloved hand over mine and squeezed so very, very lightly. I could feel heat coming through her glove. *In God's name*, I thought, *what has she done?*

"Let's be sure to keep in touch," she said. "I'm sure I'll be seeing both of you soon. Goodbye."

"Freda—" I began.

She held up a finger to her lips. "Please don't—don't say anything," she said, set her jaw firmly, then smiled.

We watched her walk to the front of the store. Before she left, she turned to us, and waved. Her smile was radiant, but it wasn't fooling me. I had looked into her eyes. Then she was gone.

Mr. Schultz came up and told me to place an ad in the paper for a full-time employee. Freda, he said, had quit. Just quit like that, no notice at all.

"I offered to raise her salary," he told us, "But she said that wouldn't be necessary. Maybe a relative died and left her some money? I don't know. She didn't offer a reason and I didn't want to pry."

He shook his head and went back into his office. I sat down to write the help wanted ad. In a few minutes, Richard came over and stood by me.

"Do you think she—?"

"No," I replied. "I'm sure it's just like the boss said, she came into an inheritance. Or something."

He nodded. "Yeah. Yeah, you're probably right."

He wandered off, and I sat there staring into space. I kept wondering about her sudden departure, and I kept thinking about those gloved hands.

∗   ∗   ∗

Freda left town a few days later. *But not before telling me the name I wanted to know.* He and I have spoken. We're on for tonight. Now I'm really scared. He says he's not going to make it as easy as he did with her. After all, he knows the value of a dollar and I have to give him his money's worth.

MAYBE A GHOST STORY, MAYBE NOT

He thrusts his fists against the posts,
and still insists he sees the ghosts.

I don't know. This could be a ghost story, although I have finally succeeded in convincing myself that I never actually saw anything. I didn't. I couldn't have. Things like that just can't be. But maybe they can. It could also be a case of mass hysteria, but can "mass hysteria" affect only two people? All I know for certain is how I felt at the time and what I probably did not really see, and what happened later when I told the story to my friend. Maybe you'll get the same feeling after you read this.

Several years ago, I went to England for two weeks and rented a car, touring all over Cornwall and Dorset, and staying at various bed and breakfast establishments. A charming little village in Cornwall, called Upper Swales, caught my fancy, and I stayed there for three nights. My hosts were an outgoing and friendly couple, and I had a number of fascinating conversations with them about the history of the village and the outlying area.

It was my last night with them (and my last night in England), and they had one more story to tell. It was a true story and had actually happened to a friend of theirs who was the rector of the local church. But before they began relating it, they ascertained that I could take ghost stories in stride and not be bothered by them. I told them I had loved stories like that ever since I was little, and asked them to proceed with theirs.

The actual event had taken place about a dozen years earlier, but my hosts had only known about it a short time, as the rector had kept it to himself for years, for fear of creating a panic or not being believed. He took only them into his confidence, and here is the story they told me:

One day in the middle of the week, the rector had been in the church, tidying things up, sweeping, dusting and getting ready for the next Sunday's service. When he had finished, he went up to the Communion rail in front of the altar to pray before departing. His back was to the pews. As he knelt there in contemplation and thought, he slowly became aware of a growing sense of unease within himself. This unease got stronger and more powerful, and the rector could no longer concentrate on his prayer. Was he experiencing the beginning of an illness? A heart attack, or a stroke? Still in a kneeling posture, he got an idea in his mind, one that he could not ignore or explain away. He gradually became absolutely convinced that some sort of malevolent presence was standing a few feet in back of him. The sudden shock and fear he felt prevented him from looking back to see if it was truly there. But he had a perfect picture of this evil phantasm in his brain. And as he told his friends years later, it wasn't so much the raw ugliness of the creature that frightened him, as it was the overpowering sense he had of its malevolent intent.

At some point he tried to force himself to turn around and confront this horrible apparition, but he simply couldn't do it. He knew he would be driven mad if he looked into its dark face.

So he did the only thing he knew to do.

He prayed.

He still doesn't remember, my hosts told me, how long he remained in prayer, or even the words he prayed. All he was aware of was that all of his heart, mind, body and soul went into that prayer. He said he felt as if he had entered into some other consciousness, some other world or dimension. It wasn't a bad feeling. It was "different," he said—and indescribable.

Time passed, and he began to return to himself, to the place, to the situation. And as strongly as he had felt the evil presence before, he now knew without a doubt that it was no longer there.

That was when he gathered up all his reserve of strength, and turned around. Of course there was nothing there, and he offered up another prayer, this one of thanksgiving for his deliverance. But as he got up to leave, something on the floor caught his eye. The floor that he had swept clean earlier. He bent down to pick it up, then dropped it as if it had burned his fingers.

A claw.

And where that claw is now and what was done with it, the rector has adamantly refused to reveal.

As soon as my hosts came to the end of that story, I realized I had been holding my breath for a very long time. As I let it out, I suddenly had the most inexplicable urge to scream as loudly as I could and run away. It was all I could do to contain myself. I had gotten too involved with the story, I told myself, and I imagined it was actually happening to me. That's all it was.

Right.

Well, I couldn't leave the town the next day without stopping in to have a look at the church.

It was unlocked, so I went in. It was a typical Norman church, with plain glass windows that were wavy from the centuries they had been in place. There were the usual memorials to past parishioners on the walls, and stone markers on the floor, denoting those who rested peacefully or otherwise beneath my feet. I had never felt quite right about treading on them, though it was unavoidable. I wondered about them, what sort of people they had been, did they still have living descendants, and more morbidly, what they thought about—if they thought—down in their eternal dark resting place.

I was the only visitor in the church, so I went freely about with a well-written history of the structure, taking note of the extreme age of the church, and that it had been built on the site of a former Roman temple.

It wasn't long before I found myself at the kneeler of the Communion rail, where the rector had had his fateful encounter. I don't know why I did it—because I truly had been frightened by the story—but I knelt there and waited. I didn't pray. I don't know if I was hoping to make something happen, or if I was just being foolish. Many minutes went by. Nothing. No weird feelings or sensations. Either the rector had had a once-in-a-lifetime experience, or his imagination had been over-stimulated. I couldn't help feeling a little disappointed, though I'm certain if I had been aware of anything not quite—right—I would have broken the world record in hasty retreats.

It was time for me to leave for the airport. I put some money in the charity box at the front door and turned around for one more look.

And I saw part of a bloody, clawed appendage dangling over the top of one of the pews. It was moving slightly, as if it were beckoning to me. *Do come over here, my dear,* I could imagine it saying, *and let's get acquainted. I want to know you better. Let's hold hands.*

I don't remember much of anything after that, just of driving like the wind to Heathrow and boarding my flight. I didn't think. I couldn't think. I wouldn't let myself. I feared for my mental status if I allowed myself to remember.

During the 8-hour plane trip back to the States, I fought with my disbelief, fought for my sanity. At last I came to a conclusion I could live with: that I had seen nothing in that church except what my overactive brain, stirred up by the rector's story, had caused me to see. The typical ghost story is usually based on an urban myth, but this one had happened to a real person. Because of that, I reasoned, I had talked myself into seeing that—that—whatever it was (*but it* was *a claw, dear God, I* know *it was, and it was dripping blood, I swear*). That figment of my imagination. Yes, that was logical and right. And after I got home, and had time to really think things through, I knew I would eventually come to laugh at myself and my suggestibility.

*   *   *

It felt good to get home, unpacked and re-settled into my usual routine once again. The "incident in the church," as I came to think of it, was never very far from my thoughts, and I became mostly convinced that I had seen nothing at all. Mostly. But not completely.

About a week after my return, I called my best friend Marie. We had been close since high school, roomed together in college, and had maintained our friendship in the decade since. When we were younger, we took great delight in watching monster movies, telling ghost stories, and scaring ourselves silly. We even competed to see who could tell the goriest tale. Whoever screamed first was the loser, and had to think up the next gruesome story.

She came over that evening, and as we sat sharing a bottle of wine, she asked how I had enjoyed my trip to England. After I had given her the highlights, I told her that I had saved the best for last, and warned her to prepare to hear something unusual. I was being overly dramatic, perhaps, but I wanted her to understand something of what I had felt. I just didn't realize the extent to which she would, or the very weird effect the story seemed to have on its listeners.

I tried to relate it in the same way I had heard it, and her ever-widening eyes told me she was riveted from my first words. Her breathing was shallow. She didn't even blink. When I got to the end of the rector's part of the story, she clapped both hands over her mouth, but could not completely stifle an agonized scream. And I must confess that I once again had the urge myself to shriek and run. How could a simple ghost story—or maybe not a ghost story—do this to its hearers?

After we had both calmed down some, she told me that while I was telling her the story, she immediately sensed that something very bad was in the room with us. She was a little embarrassed about how she had reacted, but I reassured her that I had reacted the exact same way the first time I heard it.

Since Marie had gotten so upset about what I had just related to her, I chose not to tell her the rest of it—the part about my going to the church the next day. She wasn't ready, mentally or emotionally, to hear it, and I certainly was not eager to hear myself talk about it. Not that I thought she wouldn't believe me, but I still needed time to process what I had maybe—or maybe not—seen.

With a little more wine to bolster our spirits, our moods eventually lifted, and before Marie left for home that evening, we were back to laughing and cracking jokes. I saw her to the door, said goodnight, and locked it behind her. Not twenty seconds later, the doorbell rang. It was Marie again. Her face was completely bloodless and she was on the verge of collapsing. I helped her sit down and could only watch helplessly as she gasped and gulped. I felt terrible. Obviously, my story had truly traumatized her and I tried to apologize. I got her a glass of water, but she refused it.

After a few minutes, she was able to speak. "I found this on your front porch step," she quavered.

She held out a trembling hand and opened it.

In her palm lay a claw.

*   *   *

I'm going back to England next summer, back to Upper Swales, back to the church. I must.

But I'm not going alone.

JEEPERS CREEPERS

You can discover what your enemy fears most
by observing the means he uses to frighten you.

Eric Hoffer 1902-1982

I don't scare easily. I can read Stephen King into the wee hours of the night. I can sit through *The Silence of the Lambs*, *The Exorcist*, *Alien*, *Signs*—you name a scary, gory movie and I have probably seen it. Twice. And I'm talking alone here, nobody but me in the house, late at night. I'm tough. I can take it.

I attribute my unflappability to a number of things: a difficult childhood—which I won't go into here, as I have already worked through it with an excellent therapist—an abusive ex-husband to whom I was married for twelve years, and the pride of knowing that I finally claimed the power to turn things around for myself. I went from being a timid, fade-into-the-wallpaper child, who later became a cringing, ducking and dodging wife, to at last evolving, slowly and painfully, into who and what I am now—an intelligent, strong, and independent woman who knows exactly where she stands and won't ever again let bad things sneak up behind her.

But there is one chink in my armor.

As soon as the sun begins to disappear over the horizon, I must pull down the blinds, draw the curtains, and make my house impervious to what I fear most: a Peeping Tom. It's not a matter of choice. I am compelled to do this. I can't not.

I had a bad experience when I was a young child. I was not old enough to go trick-or-treating one Halloween night. In fact, I was too young to even grasp the concept. All I have is a searing memory of innocently playing with my toys in the living room one night, when a sudden rapping at the window made me look up. Peeking, leering and goggling at me was the most heart-stopping, terrifying assortment of monsters I could ever have imagined. No nightmare could have been worse. I let out a ghastly howl of pure horror and shock. My mother came running and quieted me down. Eventually, she was even able to get me to help her drop candy into their bags, once I had been reassured that there were only children underneath the masks and costumes.

But the memory of that trauma has stuck with me and followed me into adulthood. It wasn't so much the Halloween

boogeyman I was afraid of. It was the idea of being looked at
without my knowledge, without my permission. The idea that I
could be doing anything—watching television, getting
dressed, feeding the cat—totally unconscious of the fact that
someone was watching my every move. The contemplation
of it chilled me to my very soul. The sense of violation, of
personal trespass, the rape of my privacy—that's the chink,
that's my weakness.

I have learned to live with it over the years. I have made
accommodations and compromises. To their credit, my friends
have been completely understanding about my never going
out with them at night. I have tried to laugh or shame myself
out of it. I've worked with my therapist about it, but the fear,
rational or not, just won't go away. She did suggest that I take
up a hobby to occupy my mind whenever I get overly anxious,
which I did. And it has helped—some. But nevertheless, I'm
pretty well resigned to the fact that I'll be dragging this heavy
chain of dread around with me for the rest of my days.

And the strange thing is, I have never actually *been* the
victim of a Peeping Tom.

At least I hadn't been, until three weeks ago.

I live in a house that's over 100 years old. I bought it a
few years ago with some of the inheritance money I received
from my parents' estate. The minute I saw it, I fell in love
with it. The rooms are old-fashioned, some small, others large,
and the ceilings all very high. I have truly moved my heart
and my soul into this house. It's my refuge, my rock, and my
shelter during good times and bad. It has so much Victorian
charm that I had never felt any desire to modernize it, but
last year, I did have a modest sunroom built that extends off
the back entrance to my bedroom. I chose not to change the
original door that opens into the addition, because it is a work
of art in and of itself—solid birds eye maple, golden and
glowing, sturdy and beautiful. After the construction was
completed, I was delighted to discover that the sun, when it
reaches a certain point in the sky in the afternoon, sends a

bright shaft of light through the polished brass keyhole. Not surprisingly, the key to that old lock had been lost at some point in the house's history, so the builders installed what they described as a nearly impregnable deadbolt lock. Nearly? I didn't care much for that word, but my friends reassured me that the neighborhood in which I live has always been quiet and safe. So I thought it would be all right. I had my house, and my house had me, and as long as there were blinds and curtains enough to shield me from my worst fear, my life seemed "nearly" perfect.

I was able to take early retirement from teaching English at the junior college in my town last year, and I was still trying to adjust my mind and body to my new schedule of—no schedule at all. It was difficult for the first few months. I had been used to a stable, no-surprises regimen, and it almost seemed wrong that I could now sleep late or get up early no matter what day it was. I could go to the grocery store in the middle of the morning, instead of rushing through the aisles and grabbing food off the shelves at the end of a long teaching day. I had more time for my hobbies and volunteer work. If I felt like going to a movie in the middle of the afternoon, I did. Or I could sit around all day drinking coffee in my bathrobe if I so chose, though I never was able to make myself do *that*. Old habits were hard to break, so it wasn't long before I found myself slipping into a self-imposed, but much looser, routine. A routine I felt comfortable and productive with. I still would not go out after dark, but was resolved to keep working on that.

I would usually get up around 7:00 AM, make coffee and toast, and then my cat Stirfry (he's a mixture of colors and patterns, hence the name) and I would retire to our beautiful new sunroom and watch nature as it came to life all around us. After I put a large birdfeeder in front of one of the windows, Stirfry was in heaven. That cat would have made a lethal hunter—he's very quick to sense movement or a change in the light—and he would hold himself so still as he watched a bird that I could barely tell he was breathing. Thank goodness he was a thoroughly spoiled and fat indoor cat, or I would not have had a single bird or squirrel in my yard to look at.

After breakfast, I'd take a shower and get ready for my day. If it was a Friday, I always cleaned the bathrooms and kitchen, saving the rest of the house for Saturday. Monday was errand-running day. Tuesday, I sometimes went to the crafts store to buy yarn or look at a new pattern. I considered Wednesday still to be what my students called "hump day"— I made that into my own personal free day, where I could do anything I felt like. And Thursday—well, I'm ashamed to say what I did on that day. Every Thursday, I compulsively examined and checked every single set of window blinds and curtains in the house. Scrutinized them for holes or signs of wear. Made sure that they covered every square inch of the window. If they didn't look right, I replaced them immediately. I got to be quite the handywoman at installing them. I even bought myself a rechargeable screwdriver for reinforcing curtain rods. I tried to make a joke of it and called Thursday my "Day of Safety" and tried not to feel too foolish about it. But deep down, I did. Would I never be able to rid myself of my phobia about Peeping Toms?

So that brings me to what happened three weeks ago.

It was a Wednesday, I recall. Stirfry and I got up at our usual time. It was a gorgeous May morning, and after breakfast, I prepared to sit in the sunroom for a couple of hours with a new book a friend had recommended. Stirfry settled himself in a puddle of sunshine on the floor and almost went to sleep. I say almost, because all of a sudden, his head rose, and his tail twitched like mad. Obviously, there was a "disturbance in the force," at least in his little world. He got up, trotted purposefully to one of the windows and bent his head as if watching something directly on the ground below. He maintained that posture for so long that finally I got up, too, to see what he was staring at. *Oh, no, don't let it be a dead bird*, I thought. Every so often birds would fly into one of the windows, and usually they were able to shake it off and recover. But sometimes they didn't, and I hated having to dispose of their poor broken bodies. I looked over Stirfry's shoulder, as it were, and couldn't see a thing.

"Ok, Stirfry," I sighed. "You've got *my* curiosity up now. I'm going out there, and it better be something good." (Don't you talk to your cats, too?)

I opened the screen door to step onto the small deck. I looked at the area below the window where Stirfry was still keeping watch. I didn't see a thing.

"Hey, Stirfry, you're slipping. There's nothing here to—"

But there *was* something. Something I might never have noticed if it had been a cloudy day. The month before, I had planted an herb garden beneath the window. It got lots of good light, and the plants were coming along well. At least they had been. Now some of them had been mashed into the ground. My spine was one solid icicle as I walked closer to the window. I looked down upon the plants.

Right in the middle of them was a set of footprints. And not small ones, either.

I'm dreaming, I thought. *Those aren't really here. I'll wake up any second now with Stirfry on my chest, yammering at me to get him his cat crunchies—*

But it was no use. I knew very well that I wasn't dreaming. As I stared at them, I knew that they were a man's footprints, and that they were facing directly towards my window.

*   *   *

"Would you like a refill, officer?" I asked the policeman who was sitting with me in the kitchen. After I had frantically called the police department, I had tried to calm myself down, both mentally and physically, by making a pot of good strong coffee. But there were coffee grounds scattered here and there on the counter and floor, mute testimony to how much my hands had been, and still were, shaking.

"No, thank you, ma'am," he said. Officer Timothy Snowe, who had responded to my call, set his cup down on the kitchen table and cleared this throat.

"Now here's the thing, Ms. Forrest. I don't have any doubt at all that someone was standing in front of that window trying to look in. But we can't go out and bring in every man that's got that size shoe, you see what I mean? What we *can* do is send a patrol car out to this neighborhood more frequently, especially at night. I can see by your face that you're not happy with this, but there's just nothing else we can do at this time. Our hands are tied. What I suggest is that you stay alert, keep your shades pulled down, and report anything that doesn't look right. That's the best way for help *us* to help *you*. Does that make sense?"

"Yes—it makes sense, but you see, I'm, I'm terribly, morbidly afraid of Peeping Toms. It's childish, I know. It's silly for a grown woman to—I really feel stupid!"

"You're not stupid to be afraid, ma'am. Not at all. It's the most natural thing in the world to feel fear when we see something that threatens our homes or ourselves. The thing about Peeping Toms is that they are basically not violent. They just want to look. See, they sort of get off on—uh—" He cleared his throat again. "Well, never mind. I don't want you to worry about anything. Like I said before, if you see anything funny, don't hesitate to call one of us out. That's what we're here for. Here's a card with my numbers on it— you can call the non-emergency number if you want, or 911. Keep it handy, ok?"

"I will. And thank you for coming out so quickly, Officer Snowe."

Over the next few days, I was a paranoid wreck. I kept the shades pulled down 24 hours a day. I even used duct tape to seal little openings where somebody could peek through. Every morning, as soon as it was full daylight, I would walk around outside the house and compulsively check for more footprints. I didn't see any more. I hoped that meant that the Peeping

Tom was done with me. Or, the very scared part of me whispered in my heart, maybe he was scuffing the dirt over to conceal his tracks. I prayed it was the former. It was not.

On the following Saturday night, around 9:30 or so, I was watching a movie on television and I thought I heard something outside on the front porch. I quickly turned down the volume and crept over to the living room window. I didn't have the courage to peek around the blinds, but I did turn on the porch light, and that was when I saw his shadow. There was a man at my window. A Peeping Tom looking in my window. Looking at me as I watched my movie in my bathrobe and slippers, with Stirfry on my lap. As soon as he saw the light, he instantly turned and ran off the porch and into the night. I heard the sound of something heavy being knocked over, which turned out to be a large pot of geraniums on the porch step. I stumbled to the phone to call the police. I dialed 911—*the hell with the non-emergency number*, I thought. My heart was hammering so hard that I had trouble talking, and the 911 operator had to ask me to repeat myself several times before he could understand me. Within five minutes, two policemen had arrived—Officer Snowe from my first call, and his partner, Officer Jim Rosen.

While Officer Rosen explored around outside with a flashlight, Officer Snowe stayed with me to take my statement. I was in such a state of shock, it was a wonder he could get any sense from me at all. The other officer came in a few minutes later.

"Well, there is some evidence out there that he checked out a couple of your other windows before he came onto the porch. There are footprints, but they're too faint to really tell anything. And I found some dirt on the sidewalk."

"Can you pull up any sort of clear imprint from his shoes?" I asked hopefully. Not for nothing am I an avid detective story fan.

"Afraid not, Ms. Forrest. It's all mixed up, nothing we'd be able to get any prints from. And I should tell you that this isn't the first complaint about 'looky-loos' we've had tonight from this area. A couple of your neighbors have called in, too. Looks to me like you've got yourself a real determined Peeping Tom."

Officer Snowe saw me turn pale, and jumped in to stop his partner from alarming me any further.

"That's right, ma'am, what my partner says. You are not being singled out by this sicko. It's not just you, it's everybody around here. You're not alone."

"Yeah, he's an equal opportunity Peeper, that's for sure," said Officer Rosen.

Officer Snowe scowled at his partner. "Will you shut up? Can't you see she's frightened to death? I'm sorry, Ms. Forrest," he said. Then the two officers became all business again. They finished interviewing me, told me to lock up tight, keep all curtains closed, call if I heard anything, etc. *Right*, I thought, *like that would never occur to me.*

As I watched their patrol car drive away, I felt somewhat reassured by the fact that I wasn't the only neighbor being watched by this horrible person. And I did trust that the police would do everything they could to catch him. But sometimes things just happen, and there's no one there to help. I shivered involuntarily. I felt very alone, very afraid, and very unsafe.

*   *   *

After that, I stayed in my house. Literally. I didn't step outside for an entire week. I had my groceries delivered. I called the office where I do volunteer work to tell them that I would not be there that day. I called some of my neighbors and we commiserated with each other about this awful thing going on. Since I wouldn't go out with them, my friends had been coming over to visit, so I at least had a social outlet. I couldn't go to my knitting class either, but I had previously laid in a plentiful stock of yarn. I kept myself busy so that I would not think about what was happening. I cleaned a different part of the house every day; I caught up on novels and movies on tape; I listened to music; and I worked on the sweater I was knitting for Stirfry. (I know, but in the winter he just *looks* cold.) In fact, I had finished the thing, and I had him cornered in my bedroom so I could see how, or if, it would fit, when a funny thing happened.

It was a beautiful sunny afternoon. But there was something a little bit off. I couldn't put my finger on it, but there was something. I didn't have time to wonder about it for long, as my attention got distracted when Stirfry ran away from his fitting. My shirt was a solid mass of cat hair from trying to hold him, so I took it off. Some of the hair stuck to my face, and I decided to take a shower.

Ten minutes later, I was back in the bedroom getting dressed. I had only gotten my bra and panties on when I realized what it was that didn't feel right. It was the time of day when the sun always comes flooding through my Victorian keyhole. *And there was no sun.* I looked out the window. Bright sunshine out there, but none in here. I couldn't understand what was going on. As I walked over to the door, it never, not even for one second, occurred to me what it might be.

I knelt down and put my eye to the keyhole . . .

Imagine you are standing in the middle of a busy highway, and there is an eighteen-wheeler headed straight for you, but you are unable to move your feet to get out of its path. Or that you are in the ocean and have swum past your endurance and know you have only one last bit of air in your lungs and after that is gone, you will drown. Imagine being incapacitated and forced to watch the person you love best in the world being tortured and all you can do is listen to the screams of pain and agony and terror. Imagine your worst nightmare coming true and you are powerless to wake up.

. . . and as I looked through it, I saw an eye looking back at me.

The world exploded and shattered around me. There was no noise, no smells, no sense of anything but what I was seeing. I couldn't feel the floor under me. I couldn't feel my arms and legs. Milliseconds became minutes and minutes turned into hours. All I saw, all I knew, all I was, all that had ever been or would be, was that eye looking back into mine. Then, thankfully, consciousness came crashing back into me. I could not speak, I could not scream. I could only whisper to the eye, "You—get—out—of—here." And once again I heard the sound of footsteps running away, and I slumped down on the floor, stunned and dazed.

*   *   *

The police came and did their thing and left. I kept insisting, somewhat wildly, I'm sure, that I could identify that eye, that it was burned into my brain forever, that I would never forget what it looked like. But no matter how many times I told them that, they gently but firmly said that they could not convict someone based on just an eye. "An eye ID," one of them joked. I was definitely unamused. They would have to catch this person in the act, they said, and they believed that they were closing in on him, that it was just a matter of time before he made a fatal mistake. And as they were leaving, they said they hoped I would take a little comfort from the fact that I must have given the guy as big a fright as he had given me. I didn't.

I spent all of the next day in bed, with Stirfry either on me or at my side. I called a couple of the neighbors and asked them to start a phone chain so everyone could know what had happened. I spoke with a close friend who was so supportive and empathetic, that I cried during most of our conversation. She asked how long it had been since I'd last seen my therapist and suggested that I give her a call. I did, and we ended up having an hour's session by phone.

After I had haltingly, painfully, and tearfully told her about everything that had happened to me, my therapist praised me.

"For what?" I asked. "Staying in bed all day because I'm scared of my own shadow?"

"No," she replied patiently. "Don't do that to yourself, Amelia. I know you know better than that. You showed a lot of courage. I am so proud of you. There was a time, you may remember, when you wouldn't have been able to whisper 'you get out of here' to save your life. Ok, so maybe you whisper it *this* time, but next time—and I pray there is not a next time—you will be able to scream it at the top of your lungs. You are stronger than you know. Are you hearing me? Stronger than you know."

"Thanks for your faith in me. I'm feeling a little better. Now I need to start working on putting myself back together. I can't stay in the house all day, like I'm holding my own self hostage."

She hesitated for a moment, then asked me what I thought was an odd question.

"How are you coming along with your new hobby? Is it helping to take your mind off of things for a little while? I believe you took up knitting?"

"Um, yes, that's right. I'm taking a class in it, and in fact, I just finished making a—"

She interrupted, which was not like her at all.

"Knitting—well, Amelia, that's wonderful. That's a very useful craft to know. I'm sure you'll find *lots* of different things you can do with that."

"I suppose so. I guess I can . . . Hey, maybe I could knit you a scarf or—oh. *Oh.*" I stopped abruptly.

"Yes," she said. "Yes, well, just think about it. I don't want you to be afraid anymore. I see that our time is nearly up. Let's plan on talking next week, all right? And I'm expecting to see you rather than talking to you by phone, all right?"

"Ok," I said feebly. Then in a stronger voice, "Yes, ok."

*   *   *

The very next day I got out of bed and got back into my regular activities. Began living my life again. Officer Snowe called during the week to check on me. I told him I was recovering from my shock, but that it wouldn't be long before things went back to the way they were before the Peeping Tom came into my life. He said they still planned on frequent drive-bys and that I should call anytime I got scared. I thanked him for all that he had done, and told him that I thought my scared times were coming to an end.

As the police had said earlier, it was just a matter of time. And I could play the waiting game as well as anyone.

Every sunny afternoon after that, I hung out in my bedroom. It took the better part of two weeks, but finally, my patience paid off.

I was lying on the bed reading one afternoon, when once again, I saw that there was no light showing through the keyhole. An icy shock of fright went through me, making me tremble and shake all over, but at the same time I was aware of a place deep inside me that was *not* trembling and shaking. It was calm and steady and grimly determined.

Humming casually as though I had not a care in the world, I walked slowly over to the table by the door, and picked up what I needed. A searing white heat from the metal radiated up into my arm and into the rest of my body and made me as strong as I had always wanted to be. I saw that it was the perfect tool, in the right place, at the right time, for just the right person. *A knitting needle.*

* * *

A little later, outside, I stood looking down at him. I watched impassively as he lay there, twitching and jerking and gurgling. I nudged his head with my foot until he opened his remaining eye. The eye looked all around, then it finally focused painfully on me. I knelt and bent over him until I was only inches away from that eye. His face was bloodless and his breathing was getting more and more shallow. I was going to have to hurry.

"Hey, Cyclops!" I said. "I'm looking at you."

His eye locked onto mine.

"Peek-a-boo! I see you! Hey, you know why the Cyclops had to retire from teaching? Because he only had one pupil. Get it?"

His eye slowly became glazed, then fixed, and I was witness to what should have been his most private moment—his death. I watched and I watched and I watched until I knew I would never be afraid again.

Kipling got it right. A *lot* deadlier.

* * *

I returned to the house and called the number on the card. A few seconds passed before the call went through.

"Officer Snowe here, how may I help you?"

"This is Amelia Forrest, Officer Snowe, and, actually, I believe I can help you."

CAREFUL WHAT YOU WISH FOR

The body says what words cannot.

Martha Graham

Anyone will tell you that I am the world's nicest person. Give you the shirt off my back, the last chocolate in the candy dish, the run of my house, the run of my life.

But they will also tell you that I am the world's biggest patsy. Or as we say today, I have made the choice to be non-confrontational. Choice, nothing. I'm scared stiff when it comes to speaking up for myself. I would rather let a cockroach lay eggs in my ear than argue with someone. I will pay the full sticker price for a new car rather than dicker. I allow the men in my life to treat me, not just like a doormat, but like the dirt underneath the doormat. Anybody could— and did—get anything they wanted from me, any time, any place. I could have given Casper Milquetoast lessons in timidity. It had begun to affect every aspect of my life, and I was gradually feeling more and more depressed and hopeless.

After I had loaned a time-tested, dead-beat friend my entire income tax refund—before *I'd* even received the money—my mother put her foot down and enrolled me in an adult-education class called "Adventures in Assertiveness." I would learn how to, well, put my own foot down, and stop being everyone's victim. I protested feebly that it was probably too late for me, but all she said was, "Laura, honey. Take the damn class. Please."

So I took the damn class.

It wasn't so bad, actually. There were about fifteen or twenty of us meek souls, and I think we all felt like we were among kindred spirits. It helped knowing that I wasn't the only one who had ever gotten down on my knees and literally begged the love of my life not to leave me—even though he was an abusive alcoholic. Or married. Or a gambler. Or— well, you get the picture. We were all in the same boat, and our teacher promised us that in the course of the next six weeks, we would learn how to row those boats, strongly and well, all by ourselves.

Our instructor, Ms. Cantrip, was a petite, pretty woman in her mid-thirties. She had a quiet demeanor, but that was only on the outside. Inside, she was a plain-speaking, clear-headed, decisive person who usually got what she wanted, without resorting to shouting, guilt trips, or manipulation. I admired her from the beginning, and hoped that I would be just like her someday.

On the night of the first class, we all went around and told a little bit about ourselves, and then 'fessed up to the most non-assertive thing we'd ever done. It was a clever way to get us loosened up and less nervous. Most of us laughed at our own pathetic stories. I could not. After that was over, we went around again and each person stated his or her ultimate goal. Some hoped to be able to stand up to their parents, or to their grown children; others, to their bosses; most simply wanted to have an equal say in their relationships with their friends and spouses. When it was my turn to speak, I paused for several moments to collect my thoughts. I wanted to be as clear as possible.

"What I want," I said, "is to make people hear me. *Really* hear me, and know that it's me who's speaking. I'm tired of feeling invisible and overlooked and used. I know it's a cliché, but I want my power back. I want to feel like I have some control over—" I stopped and shook my head. "Does anyone know what I mean?" A number of people vigorously nodded their heads, and I thought I saw a small ray of hope and help for me. I was ready for the adventure of assertiveness, and couldn't wait to begin.

After that, each class began with a short discussion about the various aspects of being assertive, and then we would role-play. Sometimes it was a scenario suggested by Ms. Cantrip, sometimes it was something that had happened to one of us during the past week. After the role-playing was over, the instructor critiqued us, emphasized and praised our successes, or gently but firmly explained how we had failed to make our point. She would give us assignments to do during the week. For example: start a conversation with a total stranger; return an item to the store and ask for a refund; offer up a differing opinion about something with a friend. She urged us to be keenly observant of our behavior outside of class—to notice patterns and habits in our non-assertiveness. It was a very positive and encouraging environment, and I couldn't understand why I was absolutely, without a doubt, the worst student in the class.

I knew I wasn't stupid, but it was humiliating to watch as the others grew more and more assertive, more and more in control of their words and actions, and I—I just wasn't getting it. I was either too acquiescent or too aggressive in the role-playing situations. No middle ground. I was becoming frustrated and angry and was ready to give up. The other students were very kind and very supportive, but it slowly became obvious to me that I would never overcome a lifetime of saying yes when I really meant no. Or "of course, whatever you say" instead of "hell, no!"

It seemed the only thing I could do well was to do whatever anyone wanted me to do.

One evening after class, I stayed behind to tell Ms. Cantrip that I was dropping out of the class. She said she had already sensed how I was feeling. She was quite concerned about me, and had been waiting for me to bring it up. I told her I was completely hammered down, and all I wanted to do was to go back to my bad old way of doing things. Better the devil you know, was my thought.

"Well, Laura, if you have definitely decided to quit, I can't stop you. That's your choice. But before you give up completely," she said, "I want to tell you a few things that may help you. Would you like to go out and get a coffee with me tonight?"

I didn't think she'd be able to talk me into staying, but I agreed to the coffee, and we went to a café around the corner.

It was such a relief to be able to talk to her. She told me to call her Dora—short for Endora. She hated it. Her mother had been a big fan of *Bewitched*. We laughed about some of the ridiculous names parents bestow on their innocent offspring. I myself had known a "Waterfall" in college, and had always wondered in later years how she had coped with it.

"See, Laura, this is what you need to do more of—laugh," Dora said. "You're too serious, and I think you're taking your challenges in class too seriously as well. We all need to lighten up and laugh and speak our truths in our own unique ways. Ok, so you don't get it right now—maybe in a year or two, you will. It doesn't matter when it comes, just so it comes at all. And I want—no, I *need*—to see you laugh more."

"But how can I laugh," I asked, "When my so-called friends are taking advantage of me right and left, and they think I don't know? I'm not in control of things. *They're* the ones who're laughing, and they are laughing at *me*. I'm angry and weak at the same time, and that feels pretty awful."

"I may have a solution for you. Yes, I just might. Hmm . . ." She was lost in thought for several minutes. I was starting to feel a little uncomfortable when she suddenly came back to herself and seemed to study me with a look on her face—I don't know quite how to describe it—it was a look of both appraisal and mischief.

"Yes! I have it! I know how to get you not only to laugh, but to also reclaim some of your inner power!"

Dora clapped her hands and looked extremely pleased about something as she said this, and I wondered what she might have up her sleeve. Maybe she was going to make me watch re-runs of The Three Stooges.

"All right, I'm game," I said. "What do you want me to do?"

"First of all," she replied, "Let me ask you what your favorite number is—one or two?"

Now it was my turn to be lost in thought. I stared at her and wondered for a moment if she was making fun of me. Then I realized she would never do that—she was one of the very few people I knew who wouldn't.

"You really want to know—I don't understand—what does a number have to do with anything?"

"You'd be very surprised, Laura," she said. "Now, which will it be: number one or number two?"

"Well—I guess—if I have to choose, it'd be number two."

"Perfect!" she cried. "That's exactly the number I would have chosen for you."

This conversation was starting to get a bit too flaky around the edges for me. I was beginning to think about making up an excuse to leave, when she asked to see my right hand.

Ok, I thought. *Anything, just so I can get out of here.*

She took my hand in hers and turned it over, palm side up. Then she took her right forefinger and drew a "2" over my palm.

"Very good, Laura. All will be well. We're done."

"We are? But—but—what did we do? What happened?" I sputtered.

She smiled a secret smile.

"You'll see."

"Um, all right. I'll see—what *will* I see, if you don't mind my asking?"

She smiled again. "All I can say is that you'll know it when you see it. And it won't last forever, Laura, so use it now. Use it wisely. Don't waste it. I don't do this for just anyone. It's only for the really troublesome situations in your life."

"Please, Dora. I need to know what you did and what this is all about. I have to know."

"All right, then. I'll tell you. Come closer."

And she whispered in my ear.

Then it was my turn to smile.

Now I knew she was crazy.

Or if not crazy, then at least delusional. Great, just what I needed.

I thought it best to bring our meeting to as graceful an end as possible, so I told her I needed to get home and feed my cat. We walked back to our cars, and before she drove off, she reminded me again to use "it" sparingly and to "make it count" whenever I did. I humored her by promising I would (and humored myself by resolving to drop the class immediately). I guess I should have known—anyone who has a bumper sticker on her car that says "My other car is a broom" can't be playing with a full deck. *Oh well, live and learn*, I thought to myself.

*   *   *

As I was unlocking the door to my apartment, I could hear the phone ringing. I always felt I had to answer it. I had caller ID and an answering machine, but I could never bring myself to just let it ring and ring. I skidded around the corner and grabbed the phone.

"Hello?" I said breathlessly.

"Yes, Ms. Braithwaite?"

"Yes, it is."

"Good evening, how are you this evening, ma'am? Good, fine, I'm very glad to hear that. We would like you to take a short survey—"

A telemarketer. I never can get them stopped in time, no matter what I say.

"I'm afraid I don't have the time, but thank you for calling." I always try to be polite at least.

"Yes, ma'am, it's a very short survey, we won't take much of your time—"

"I'm sorry, I can't, but thank—"

She interrupted me and launched into her spiel, as if she hadn't heard a single word I'd said. The combination of a miserable assertiveness-training class, the discovery that the instructor was seriously weird, and the fact that I'd nearly twisted an ankle trying to get to the damn phone was suddenly too much to take. I'd had it, and I was mad!

This time I yelled. "I said no! I don't have the time! Didn't you hear me the first time?"

No response from the telemarketer. Complete silence for several moments, then she said, "Huh? What the—um—oh, dear, I've got to—*oh my God*!" and then the connection was broken.

I didn't know what had happened, but at least I could hang up.

*   *   *

It wasn't until a couple of days later that I began to understand and believe that Dora really had given me some kind of power. It was my day off. I'd planned to sleep in, have a leisurely breakfast, then perhaps spend the afternoon shopping. But at precisely 5:00 AM, the neighbor's dog started barking. And barking. And barking. This had happened a lot since the family had moved in a few weeks earlier, and I just couldn't bring myself to ask them to please keep their dog inside so I could sleep. I'd start to walk over there, then turn tail and run for home. Then I would try to compose a polite letter to them, but could never send it. I felt helpless—again a victim of my own cowardice. But getting waked up before it was barely light—well, this time, it was just too much. I felt unaccustomed anger welling up inside me, and before I realized what I was doing, I had opened the window and was yelling at the dog to shut up. He looked up at me and, just for a moment, something strange seemed to pass between us. When I thought about it later, it was like a sort of force had burst out of me and gone straight for the dog. And after I'd shouted at him, the dog did quiet down. Actually, he couldn't bark for—I don't know any other way to put it—pooping. He suddenly squatted where he stood and just kept doing it. I never saw so much—you know what—come out of a small dog like that. A few minutes went by, then the door opened and the owner came out. When he saw what, and how much, his dog had done, he scooped the dog up and went back into the house. Just before he went in, he looked up at me and gave me a dirty look, as if *I'd* been to blame for the dog's overabundance of—oh, surely not. I couldn't have caused anything like that to happen. I couldn't override Nature. That would be, you know, unnatural. But then I remembered the telemarketer incident, and for a moment, I wondered. Dora couldn't really have—could she? But rational thought returned, and I chalked the two things up to coincidence.

That same night, my mother and I went to a movie. I told her about why I was no longer taking the assertiveness course, and she said she understood. I don't know if she really did, since I didn't bring up the strange thing Dora had done, but that's the good thing about my mother—she knows when to back off and not push. And she *said* she could see a difference in my demeanor from the several classes I had gone to, but again, I think she was being kind. I certainly didn't feel different, just a little puzzled about the two recent incidents.

After the movie started, we realized that we were sitting in front of some talkers. Mother looked back casually and whispered to me that it was two middle-aged women. They were discussing an upcoming party at great length and detail. I tolerated it for a while. Just for a while. Then I decided, all right, I'll see if I can politely but assertively *ask* them to be quiet. I turned towards them, but again didn't have the courage to say anything. But as I tried to pay attention to what the actors were saying in the movie, I just could not concentrate for all the dialogue going on behind us. Irritation, annoyance, and finally, anger washed over me. This time I knew I could do it. I turned around to fuss at them, but before I could speak a word, they both suddenly sat bolt upright, their eyes big with shock. "Jesus," one of them whispered. "I have to get out of here!" said the other. They jumped up and stumbled over people in their race to reach the aisle. They hit the door running, and did not return. But for several minutes, there was bit of a smell—no, a positive stench that they had left behind them. But it was quiet. Definitely quiet. And my mother and I watched the rest of the movie in peace.

Afterwards as we walked to the car, she praised me for what I'd done.

"That class has done you more good than you give yourself credit for, Laura," she said. "What in the world did you say to them?"

"Oh, well—I just, um, asked them to please be quiet or have the courtesy to go."

"Well, it was very effective, but I wonder why they felt that they had to leave. All they had to do was sit there and not talk."

"I don't know," I said. "Maybe they were embarrassed or something."

Mother pondered a moment.

"Well, it was obvious that one of them had—had passed a little wind—but that's no reason to leave."

As we drove away, my mind was in a tumult. I was beginning to think that it was more than just "a little wind," and that I had caused it.

*   *   *

I shifted uneasily in the pew and crossed and uncrossed my legs for about the twentieth time since the minister had begun his sermon. Would he never finish? I surreptitiously glanced at my watch. He'd been going for forty minutes, and he wasn't even close to winding it up. I saw other people getting restless, too, and a couple of them even got up and left. I'd never have the nerve to do that. That might hurt the minister's feelings, and I always went out of my way to spare others' feelings. *But wait a minute*, I thought, *what about* my *feelings? My time?* I had plenty of things to do that day—laundry, dishes, cleaning the house, getting ready to begin another work week—but I was pinned down here, at the mercy of a man who barely knew my name. What could I do? Then I thought—but, no, I couldn't really make that happen at will. Or could I?

Well, all I could do was try.

I knew the very instant that it happened. One moment, he was droning on about Revelations; the next, he stiffened and said all at once, "MaytheLordblessyouand-keepyouAmen." As he stepped—no, leaped—down from the pulpit, he motioned for the junior minister to take over, and he exited, stage left, apparently pursued by bears. The church service wound up in a timely manner after that, and as I drove home, I knew without a doubt that Dora had given me a gift—a very unique and strange one, to be sure—but a gift all the same. And she had given me something else, too. I remembered the old joke about "he who farts in church must sit in his own pew," and I started to titter, then giggled, then laughed, and finally guffawed all the way home. Dora had given me my laugh back!

That evening, I looked up Dora's name in the phone book and called her. The instant she heard my voice, she asked, "So, Laura, are you laughing now?"

"Well, yes, I certainly am," I said. "But Dora, I'm very confused. How did you—what did you do to me? Did you hypnotize me? Is it a spell of some kind? Is this real? I mean, *who are you?* Are you some kind of wi—I beg your pardon, Dora, it's just that I'm so overwhelmed by all this. But are you . . . ?"

I could not make myself say the word. I wanted to know, but at the same time, I didn't. Besides, that word might not be the politically correct one, and I really didn't want to offend her. Not after having seen what she had done for me.

"Are you having fun, Laura?" she asked.

"Yes, I guess so. But am I really and truly making people— you know, right then and there, in their pants? This isn't a dream?"

"It's no dream, Laura. It really doesn't matter what I call myself and my art, does it? I do it for the people I like, the ones who I see struggling, and need a little extra boost. Like you. I enjoy helping. It brings me pleasure to know I can really make a difference in their lives. And you can't deny that your life is different now, can you?"

"No," I said. "It's definitely different, that's for sure. Well, uh, how long can I go on doing this? Is there a time or person limit? I mean, I don't want to go crazy with it. But you know that I've got some real—some real assholes in my life, and they deserve . . . why are you laughing? Oh, I get it." And we both howled at my terrible Freudian slip.

"Laura, all I can tell you is that this power won't last forever. I can't say how long for sure. That is not given to me to know. But you will be able to feel it waning when the time comes. So, as I said before, use it wisely. You never know when the last time will be."

"I've used it four times already."

"Then I would say that you'd better start making the remaining ones count."

"I will," I promised. "Thank you, Dora, for this. For making me feel powerful and strong."

"I only gave you the key, my dear. *You* are the one creating all the power and strength inside you."

"Oh, wow. I never thought of it that way. Me, powerful and strong? I never would have dreamed such a thing."

I felt myself on the verge of tears, so I joked, "Well, I'd better go. So many assholes, so little time, right?"

Dora hung up laughing.

* * *

As I thought about my new "gift" over the following week, I had a strong, inner-voice feeling that I probably had about three, maybe four more opportunities left in me. So I began making a list. I called it my "Kick Ass and Take Names" file. First I put every name on there I could think of, and then I started paring it down. I finally ended up with the names of four people who had, at one time or another, purposefully and deliberately manipulated, deceived, and insulted me, or had taken base advantage of my kind and innocent nature.

My first impulse was to run out, hunt each one down, and pay them back in my own new special way. But reason won out—I wanted to stretch this out for as long as I could. So I decided that one person per week until I ran out of gas—ha ha—would just about do it. That way, I could enjoy the moment, while anticipating the next one. And I decided against doing it to annoying little dogs. That hadn't been fair to the poor thing. It was his owner who really deserved what I had begun to call "the Power of Poop."

But I did know the one I wanted to save for last: my former—and I use the term loosely—boyfriend. He had certainly not been a friend, or a man in any sense of the word. He had been all attention, flowers, and candy and tenderness at the beginning, and then when he felt sure of me, he began to treat me like—well, like what I was planning to do to him. I can't believe how long I put up with his lies, his apologies and excuses, his infidelity, his "this-time-I'm-really-going-to-leave-my-wife-for-you-baby."

Yes. I had a couple of fun weeks to look forward to, and I thought I would most likely be laughing myself back into good mental health in no time at all.

Monday morning was payback time for a woman I worked with. We'd had an on-again, off-again type of friendship for several years. I didn't like her, but could never say no to her invitations to go out. I would kick myself the next day for having accepted, but as usual, felt helpless to do anything about it. She was a sneaky one—the type who manages to get in some subtle but sharp digs while looking and sounding completely innocent. There was never anything concrete I could point to and accuse her of. It always ended in my feeling criticized and demeaned. But the worst part of it was something that had happened recently. I had made the mistake of mentioning to her an idea that I planned to talk over with the office manager. Not only did she take my idea and run with it to the manager, but she took full credit for it and intimated that it was too bad that it was always on her shoulders to come up with good ideas, and that perhaps the rest of us ought to at least try and pitch in from time to time. Intolerable and insufferable! And it was going to stop today!

I was almost shivering with pleasure as I got ready for work.

As soon as I got to my office, I checked the day's schedule. Things were still going my way. There was a meeting of all the department heads and staff scheduled for just after lunch. That, I determined, was when I would strike.

And it really wasn't my fault that she chose to have chili that day for lunch. All I did was not discourage her from ordering it.

It was just as she began her report to the board that I decided it was time for her to make a hasty departure.

I'm not sure what the best part was: the way she knocked her chair over and got tangled up in the legs as she sprinted for the door; the shocked and horrified faces of everyone as they gradually realized what had happened; or how, as she left the room, a small, round piece of—how should I put it—fecal matter, rolled out from one of the legs of her pantsuit and just sat there for us all to look at and ponder upon. She had always prided herself on putting everything she had into her work. I have to say that she had certainly accomplished that, and I thought it was a job well done. I took myself out to dinner that night in celebration, and when the server asked if he could take my order, I thought he said "ordure" and it caused me to do a spit take with my water. I thought I would die laughing.

*   *   *

Over the next several days, I worked out a strategy for my next subject, but before I could act upon it, I happened to see my ex-boyfriend one Saturday night entering a dance club with a beautiful blonde on his arm. She wasn't his wife, nor was she the one he had cheated on me with. She had to have been the third or fourth one down the line, because he changed women like some people change their underwear. (I grinned when I realized that I had been causing a lot of *that* to happen lately!) I had wanted to save him for my final treatment, but the opportunity was too fortuitous to pass up. So I parked the car and followed them inside after a few minutes.

It was dark enough in the club that I wasn't worried he would see me. I had them constantly in view—I knew I'd find the exact right moment. I could tell that he hadn't known her very long. He was clearly trying to impress her, gazing deeply into her eyes, touching her hand from time to time, attending to every word she said, as though she were the only woman in his world. I should know, because he had done the same things to me. So I just bided my time. They ordered drinks, and after a few minutes, he asked her to dance. That was it, that was my signal.

I waited until they had worked themselves into the middle of the other dancers on the floor. Thank goodness, it was a slow song. He seemed to have at least four hands, the way they were moving all over her body. And I could tell she was falling for him. I couldn't let this go on any longer, so I struck. And as I did, I thought, *This is for me and for all the other gullible*

women you've duped. This is for all the nice women who have ever
been stood up, or used and abused, or dumped simply because
there was another with blonder hair or bigger breasts or more money.
This is for all of us.

I truly didn't mean to get her too. I guess the power of
my anger plowed a wider furrow than I realized. Oh well. It
might have been for the best that she be disillusioned sooner
rather than later.

When it hit them, they immediately jumped away from
each other as though they'd been shocked with electricity.
Then they began desperately to break through the crowd of
dancers, but it was slow going. Other people were now starting
to notice that there was a certain problem. That's when *they*
began backing away, but all that accomplished was to slow
things down even more. I stood there in a shadowy corner,
watching everyone's reactions with barely concealed laughter.
Some held their noses, some appeared to slip in something
on the floor. My ex and his poor date were still doggedly
making for the exit. As they passed by me, I heard her say,
"You put something in my drink, you bastard. Take me home
right now, and don't you ever call me again!" Those words
were a balm to my heart. And the look on my ex's face—
well, it was priceless. He was trying to look as if nothing at all
had happened, while at the same time, dismay and disgust
were plastered all over his face. It was a moment to treasure,
a little alloyed because I hadn't had a camera with me, but
still a good time was had by—me.

It was a little cocky of me, I know, but the next day I
mailed him an anonymous note that said: "I didn't know you
had it in you."

I was indeed getting cocky and arrogant, and I knew that
was not like me. That was not the result Dora had wanted to
create when she gave me this unusual gift. And yet—the
power to make people pay for the wrongs they had done me;
the intoxicating knowledge that I could, in a moment's whim,
cause those people to have the worst and most embarrassing

day of their lives; and the idea that I potentially had everyone under my thumb—these things made me a little heedless of what I was becoming. I could feel the gift waning in me, as Dora had said it would, and I felt a little sad that things were coming to an end. But I also felt that the power was a very dangerous thing to own, and it would be something of a relief when it was gone, since it was starting to warp who I really was inside. I made the decision then and there to not use the gift again. I would, instead, take from it those things that Dora had intended for me—a rekindled sense of humor and the ability to laugh, the realization that I would never let anyone push me around again, and the very real sense of my own authentic personal power. A power that reflected my true self. I had done it. I had graduated from the assertiveness class, and I could and would be happy with those things for the rest of my life.

I had bought Dora a little thank-you gift (a very pretty music box along with a plate of homemade fudge—again ha ha) and was driving to her house the next day to give it to her.

I live in a town where people run red lights all the time. You're taking your life in your hands if you start into the intersection when the light turns green without checking all around first. I'm a cautious driver, and I nearly always stop as soon as the light goes yellow.

I did so this time, evidently displeasing the driver behind me, who must have intended to race through the red. He began honking his horn and flashing his lights at me. Every now and then he revved up his engine, then reverted back to honking and flashing. I didn't look back, but if I had, I'm sure I would have seen The Dreaded Finger. Would this red light ever turn green and let me get out of his way? I could feel a self-righteous anger welling up in me. *I* obeyed the law, why couldn't everyone else? And here I was on the receiving end of some very bad behavior, just because I was doing the right thing.

I hadn't planned on it, but I felt the power coming out of me and wanting to go into the honker behind me. *All right*, I promised myself, *one last time*. Then it will be gone forever. No sense in wasting the last little bit, was there?

I made ready to unleash it, and raised my head in order to see the driver in my rearview mirror.

What I saw were my own eyes looking back at me.

Oops.

THE COMFORT OF GERANIUMS: MAYELLA EWELL'S STORY

DEDICATION

For Elizabeth Lee, for introducing me to Mayella.

If I can stop one heart from breaking,
I shall not live in vain;
If I can ease one life the aching,
Or cool one pain,
Or help one fainting robin
Unto his nest again,
I shall not live in vain.

—Emily Dickinson

PROLOGUE

I know what people in this town think about me and my family. I see the hate and disgust in the set of their mouths. The way they watch me out of the corners of their eyes. The way they pull back from me as though to touch me would dirty them.

Most nights, I have the same dream:

Papa and me are in the courtroom and people are looking at me. Mostly men. They smell of sweat, tobacco, liquor. I feel sick to my stomach and I'm afraid—not of being sick—but of what he's making me do. Maybe I won't do it this time. But now I'm in the witness chair, looking out at all the Maycomb folks, and I see Papa's face. I can read his lips. He's saying, "You better do it, better say it, you worthless slut, or I'll give you the strap till you can't stand up no more." I look away, and see the other one's face, and I remember how gentle and kind he was. Shame fills me, and I turn my head.

Now a tall man with spectacles is standing in front of me. He looks kindly at me and smiles. I wish for a moment I was his daughter. How different things might have been. He smiles again and says, "Miss Mayella . . . let's just get acquainted."

That's when I wake up, always in a sweat, always with the same words in my head. Maybe it's still not too late to say them.

This time I *do* have something to say, Mr. Finch, and I want to tell what happened. I want to tell the truth.

My name is Miss Mayella Ewell.

PART 1

Chapter 1

One of Them Ewells

I was born in dirt. I have lived in dirt most all my life. My mama had me on the dirt floor of our cabin because we couldn't pay for a doctor. My world was Papa's bellows when he was fighting mad, his whimpers when he was sick drunk. Mama's screams when he beat her. The rotten stink of the dump we lived next to. Not enough to eat, not enough to wear. I lived my life trying to keep us children and Mama from being near killed with Papa's strap or his fists. I cared for my mama in her sickness and wept for her at her death. I tried to keep Papa away from me and my sisters after Mama was gone. Tried to make us clean. Tried to make us anything but Ewells, and failing.

Once I nearly killed Papa, right after Mama died. I hated him enough to, and I often wish I had, because then none of the rest of it would have happened.

But I did kill a man, you know. A man I loved. I killed him with my words, then I killed him with my silence. Killed him with my fear.

I have wanted every day of my life since then to take all of it back, to make things different, make them right.

But I can't. Dead is dead, and black will never be white. I can't never make it clean, never lift it outta the dirt where it happened. It's fitting that I will live with this sorrow for the rest of my life.

Even now, years after the trial, most people in Maycomb say the Ewells was and always will be trash. That my paw was the very devil hisself (else why was he killed on Halloween, they ask). That I am a sinful, wicked girl that don't deserve to live in decent society.

I'd most likely be dead now if it wasn't for a few blessed folks who think that no one is past saving, and who will always reach a hand out to a drowning person.

I was that drowning person, and for what they have done for me, I will honor them all my life.

It was like God sent angels to lift me out of the water and put me in a place of light and goodness and love. And they have give me the chance to help another one such as me. One who must also hide from the world because of what his family is. If I can only bring a little light into his dark world, maybe . . . maybe that light will someday be enough to show me the way back to my mama in Heaven.

I'm writing this for my angels, for my mama, and for Tom.

Please, God, hear my story, and at the end, see whether I am worthy of a little understanding, a little love.

Chapter 2

Family Pictures

From the beginning, I remember the geraniums. Mama's geraniums. Their bright red flowers and the spicy smell of the dark green leaves. Mama singing around the cabin. Papa making silly faces at me so's I'd laugh, and calling me his little May-ellaphant because I'd been such a big baby. Hot biscuit and sausage gravy. Crackling bread. Squirrel stew bubbling away on the stove. Mama and Papa talking over supper, laughing, him whispering to her and her blushing and saying, "Hush, Bob, the child." Hands touching as they washed up the dishes together.

When I close my eyes, I can still see them as they was then. How young Mama was, her face lined not with sickness and worry but with smiles. How Papa'd sometimes call us "his girls," pick us both up and swing us around till we was all dizzy. They didn't hardly have two nickels to rub together, but I think they loved each other then. I was barely walking good yet, and another one was on the way. All life was ahead of us, and long as we had each other and our cozy cabin, it would be good because we was family.

But that was before the babies started coming regular, one most every year. Before their first-born son's death, before the dirt and the poverty and the drinking begun.

I have only one picture of Mama, took around the time she married Papa. She's so beautiful, so alive, barely seventeen, and her dark eyes flash back at the camera with laughter and mischief. She was tiny and it always amazed folks how many babies her little body would birth. Prettiest thing about her was her hair. "Skunk black," Papa would tease her. It was rich ebony, long and thick, and when the sun was on it, she looked like she had a dark, glossy halo. She had a time of it, though, keeping it neat—no matter how many hairpins went into it in the morning, by suppertime lots of wispy tendrils had fell down around her shoulders. She declared she was "all sixes and sevens," and then she'd go to patiently pin it all back up again. I loved to touch it when she had it down at night, and sometimes Papa would pet her like a cat.

Several months after she passed, I would keep finding her hairpins in corners or under the cot when I cleaned the cabin. I kept them in a little box I'd found in the dump. If Papa was very bad with drink, I used to put her pins in my hair. It made me feel less scared of Papa, and closer to Mama.

I still have that little box, and when I die, it will be buried with me.

I don't have no pictures of Papa—his family was too poor. He never was a big man, but was very wiry, very strong. He had pale blue eyes and his hair was a kind of sandy color. He got gray at a pretty young age, and in the last few years before he died, it was downright sparse and flyaway. Papa's face and neck was red from being outside so much, and from too much liquor. You just looked at him and knowed he'd had a hard upbringing. He never said much about it, except when he'd go to whip one of us and say, "Y'all don't know what a *real* beatin' is." We sure got lots of chances to find out. I wonder if Papa's folks had been a mite easier on him, maybe he wouldn't have drank so. Guess it don't matter much now though.

Mama's folks lived in Abbottsville, and I would go and stay with them for a week or so every year. Most times when I got back to our cabin, I had a new baby brother or sister. I loved staying with them. Grandpa had a wicked sense of humor. He'd sometimes take out his false teeth and chase me with them, clacking them together. I'd pretend to be scared, and we'd make such a noise running through the house that Grandma would declare we was going to bring the roof down around her ears. She would sound fussed, but that was only pretend too. She loved the fun and laughter as much as Grandpa and me did. I loved them both so much, especially Grandma. I didn't have her near long enough, though, and I still can't talk much about her without crying.

Both Papa's ma and pa was gone before I was old enough to remember them. From the little that Papa would say about him, his paw had been a pretty hateful person, and a mean drunk, and didn't believe in sparing the rod, especially with Papa, the oldest boy. Grandpa Ewell died not long after my folks was married. He got blind drunk one hot summer night and passed out in the middle of the road that goes to Meridien. The first car that come along run clean over him and killed him. Grandma Ewell wasn't never completely in her right mind after her husband died, and she had to be put in the state hospital in Birmingham. She had an awful death. She choked on a hunk of meat one evening at supper, and before anybody could do anything, she was stone cold. We never hardly heard much from Papa's brothers and sisters. They'd all growed up and moved away to different places. They wasn't never what you'd call close.

Maycomb folks probably was never positive how many there was of us Ewell children.

I was the oldest of eight.

There would've been nine, but one died almost before he could take breath, poor thing.

After me was my brother Robert. He was named after Papa, of course. I still couldn't talk real plain yet when he was born, and "Burris" was as close as I could get to "Robert." The name stuck, and he was called that forever after.

Then come the others: Elias, for Mama's paw; Sally; Luther; Garnet; then finally, the twins, Amelia and Miranda.

That is—was—our family. The Ewells. Spite of our name, spite of what Papa become, spite of what I done, that name will be mine forever. Because no matter what, we are family forever.

Chapter 3

Happier Days

In the years before Mama begun to get sick, and Papa took to drink, our family had some nice times, even happy times. They didn't happen often, but I was always grateful when they did. I can still call some to mind.

If Papa'd been working steady and had a few nickels to spare, he'd take us into town for ice creams if we'd been good. We didn't get such treats like this hardly ever, and we'd see who could make their ice cream last the longest. Now that I can have ice cream most any time I want, it don't taste as good as what Papa got us. He and Mama ordered the same thing every time—a strawberry ice cream soda and two straws.

We could usually get Mama to talking about how she and Papa had met over a plate of strawberry ice cream. She was visiting some kinfolk near here, and they had took her to the Baptist ice cream social in Maycomb. She was most eighteen, and Papa would've been a year or two older. She was a real pretty girl, and she caught Papa's eye right off. And Mama thought she'd never seen a finer-looking boy than Robert E. Lee Ewell. It wasn't long before he'd introduced himself. "What's the 'E' in your name stand for?" she asked as they stood in line for their ice cream. "Dunno," Papa answered with a twinkle in his eye. "My folks never told me." Well, he just kept on teasing and joking with her ("downright flirting is what he was doing," said Mama), till she declared she didn't know what to think. I guess Papa knowed what to think well enough, because they got married just three months later. And I and my brothers and sisters come along in the years after to make us a family.

In the summers when it was too hot to sleep inside, we'd sometimes go and set on the roof, hoping to catch a little breeze. We listened to the mysterious night sounds of frogs and whippoorwills, we looked at the stars and moon for hours, and we'd talk. Talk about anything and everything. My folks was real patient with our childish questions, and would answer as best they could. Why do our fingers get so wrinkly when they're in water? Why does the preacher go on so long? Why was Mama and all her sisters named for flowers? Why does grits taste better salted? At some point, one of them would say, "All right, that's enough for now." Then we would set there real quiet, till one by one, us children would get sleepy, and have to be lifted down gently by Papa into Mama's waiting arms, and put back in our cots.

Another thing I remember is that my folks both loved to sing. They had good voices. Mama's favorite hymn was "What a Friend We Have in Jesus," and Papa loved "Cotton Eye Joe." Sometimes of an evening, to make us children laugh, they'd sing their songs both at the same time, getting louder and louder, till all the words and notes was mixed up together into nonsense. They never could finish—both was laughing so much that Mama would have to sit down and fan herself for a spell, and Papa would have to be slapped on his back.

Christmas and birthdays wasn't never much to us, what with no money for gifts or a tree. But as long as I live, I will never forget the Christmas when I was seven. Mama'd been secretly saving a little outta the welfare checks, and when us children woke up that morning, the first thing we seen was Christmas stockings hanged up for each of us. We dove into them like we was afraid they was going to disappear. Well, we all of us got an orange! A whole orange of our very own!

Mama stood off aways watching us yelling and screaming, and she cried, partly to see how happy and excited we was, and partly because she knowed how much we always had to do without. I can still remember holding my orange to my cheek, its good smell, the roughness of the peel. The other children ate theirs right away, but I didn't. I took mine to bed with me that night because I wanted it to last as long as it could. I layed it on my pillow so's I could look at it and touch it and smell it whenever I wanted. I ate it slow the next day, and I kept the peel for a long time after, to remind me of my first and only Christmas present. I have gotten a few gifts since those days, but wasn't none of them as good as that wonderful orange from Mama.

These times are real nice to remember, and when Mama and Papa was getting along, I felt warm as toast inside, and I wanted it to go on forever.

But it didn't—couldn't, of course. As the years passed, there was whiskey, sickness, a baby every year, less work, less money—the good times just run out for us.

I like to think of Mama and Papa, both now in Heaven, all their anger and grief and sadness forgotten. I hope they're still laughing and singing together, and still having strawberry ice cream sodas with two straws.

Chapter 4

Learning to Love

When my folks was bringing us up, times was hard, and it was all we could do sometimes to stay warm and fed. It was that way for most everybody. And even though we knowed we was just Ewells, we was still a family, and families was supposed to love each other. As awful as my life got to be over the years, what with Mama dying, Papa's drinking and beatings, and the terrible sin I committed towards another, I hate to think how much worser things would've been if I hadn't knowed my grandma for the little time I did. She was the first and only person who ever said, right out loud, that she loved me. My folks and us never said that. I don't know exactly why. I think Mama was maybe a little shy of saying it—she showed her love in the way she took care of us. And Papa, when he worked and wasn't drinking, he brung in a little money and food, and that was how he loved us. But for us to say it to each other—well, that would've felt kinda tacky and embarrassing.

But it never embarrassed Grandma. She wasn't never afraid to say them words. And whenever I went to visit her and Grandpa, I was sure to hear them.

But whenever she did that, whenever she told me she loved me, I couldn't never say it back to her. Not that I didn't love her—I did, so much, so much. But all I could do was turn hot and red and stare down at my feet. I was so afraid that I was hurting her feelings every time I did that, but I just couldn't make myself say what she wanted to hear.

God and Grandma taught me a lesson I haven't never forgot. It was my eleventh birthday, and I'd been staying with my grandparents for a few days. On the morning I was to go home, I packed my few things and went into the front room to tell them goodbye. I hugged Grandpa, and he give me a kiss on the cheek.

"Come back as soon as you can, honey, you know we love having you here," he said. I promised him I would, if Papa was willing.

Grandma was on the settee, a quilt over her legs, as she felt the chill of the mornings sometimes. When I set down beside her, she held me in her arms as if she never would leave off, and give me a good squeeze. Then she looked into my eyes and said, "I love you so much, Mayella."

Before I even knowed I was going to do it, the words just somehow or other flew out of my mouth: "I love you, too, Grandma."

I felt shocked at myself, and very, very shy. I didn't know where to look, but Grandma lifted my chin until my eyes met hers. She looked so happy. She kissed me on the forehead, and said, "God bless you, dear."

I didn't know it then, but that would be the last time I ever saw her alive. God took her in her sleep a few weeks later.

Every day in my prayers, I thank God that He helped me make my grandma happy with them five little words. I'm so grateful that she finally knowed I loved her and could say so.

Before the funeral, I asked Grandpa to please tuck into Grandma's hands a note I had wrote for her.

It was a tiny piece of paper, but it said so much:

"I love you, too, Grandma."

Chapter 5

Mama's Geraniums

Mama always liked to say that the only things she brung into her marriage was a side of salt pork and three pots of geraniums. The pork got used up soon enough, but her geraniums still live to this day.

Red, the brightest scarlet red—that's the only color she would grow. What with our cabin being so dark, she declared that they "lighted up the house right nice."

And she was a dab hand at growing'em too. She knowed exactly when they needed watering or cutting back, where to put them so's they'd get enough light, when to start new roots from the old.

She told us children that one of the ways God loves us is with flowers, and that we must love Him back by taking care of them, and helping them to grow beautiful and strong. Mama's geraniums was holy to her, you could tell by the way she touched them.

When she was showing me how to take care of her plants, she said that tending to them was like raising a family. The new little cuttings was the babies, she explained, and you had to see to it that they got the right food and water, light, and gentle touches so that they could grow up healthy and strong. The weak ones had to be supported till they got to where they could stand on their own. Once you done them things, she said, they would be ready to go off and make their own babies, and start the whole thing all over again.

"And then," she laughed, "this old geranium here'd be a grandma, just like I'll be someday when you start in having babies, Mayella."

I was only nine or ten years old at that time, and I told her I couldn't imagine being old enough to have babies—it seemed like it was a hundred years off.

"Oh no, honey, you will someday. My little Mayella-cutting will grow up soon enough, and have lots of babies. I can't hardly wait!"

Mama was really tickled at the idea of being a grandma, and it was good to see her so happy. How sad, I think now, that neither of these things ever come true.

Then I asked her why she only liked geraniums.

"They was allus my mama's favorite," she said. "And she taught me to grow them, just like I'm teachin' you now. Besides, I like what geraniums say."

"Flowers can't talk, Mama!"

"Oh, they most positively can, Mayella. Pansies, now, they mean real nice memories. Gardenias say purity. Stock is—let me think—lasting beauty, and azaleas mean first love."

"What about your name, Mama?"

"Well, Violet means faithfulness. I wanted to call you Mayella Daisy when you was first born. Daisies mean gentleness and innocence. But Papa wanted you named after me. I think either flower suits you."

"And geraniums, Mama? What do they say?"

"Geraniums are for comfort, Mayella. They say don't grieve, don't be sad. Only look at us and be comforted by our beauty." I told her that geraniums would be my favorite flower from now on.

She kissed me, and said, "That's my good daughter."

*   *   *

Today, I am looking after my own geraniums, took and rooted from Mama's original plants.

I go to visit her grave often. I make sure the geraniums planted there are still healthy and growing. The stems are strong, and they hold up masses of dark green leaves and the brightest scarlet blooms. And I try to take comfort from them. They grow as if they knowed whose grave they was honoring.

Chapter 6

The School Dress

Us Ewell children didn't stay in school for many years. I went the longest, most three years. After I stopped going, Papa said he'd have made me quit anyways. "A girl don't need more learnin' than that," he gruffed. "Anymore'd be a pure waste. 'Sides, Mayella, your ma needs you at home."

School was hard for me. Not that I was backward—a teacher once said she thought I was right smart for a girl my age. I could read and write pretty good. No, school was hard not on account of what I didn't know, but of who I was. I was "one of them Ewells," and that was enough said for most of my teachers and the other children. Didn't matter how clear I could write, how fast I read, how quick I could do sums. I was a Ewell. I was dirt and not hardly worth the teaching.

It got so's the teachers wouldn't never call on me to recite, or even see me with my hand up to answer a question. The other pupils looked clean through me like I was glass. Sometimes I wondered if I was really a ghost, but I was the only one who didn't know it.

It didn't seem fair to me. I couldn't help being who I was, couldn't help having to wear a flour sack dress with no stockings, and cracked shoes, couldn't help not always being clean. It was hard to keep yourself washed good in our cabin. Pretty soon I stopped raising my hand in class. Nobody noticed. Some days I didn't feel up to being sneered at, so I stayed home. Nobody noticed. I would show up with bruises or even a blacked eye. Nobody said nothing, nobody done nothing.

That's what I felt like. That's what I was. Nothing.

After a while, I didn't wait for them to leave me alone. I begun to keep myself away from them. When it was noontime, I stayed at my desk and ate my lunch alone. Mama, bless her, always managed to scrounge up a cold biscuit or two and tie them in her handkerchief for me. Every morning as I left for school, she'd hand me my lunch and tell me she'd left a kiss in it, just for me. I think she knowed how I felt about going to school. That made me feel less alone, her knowing how things was with me.

I did get my studies, though, in spite of being unhappy and overlooked. I had more time to listen to the lessons, to learn, to think. I just kept it all tucked away inside of me, like Mama's biscuits in that handkerchief, and it was a special secret only I knowed about.

My first day in third grade was also my last.

A week before, Mama had found a dress about my size in the dump. It was some worn, but not too dirty, and as a surprise for me, she worked on it nights after I'd went to bed, mending and cleaning it, making it over so's it'd fit me.

First day of school, she give it to me. "You don't hardly ever get presents, Mayella, but I want you to have this because you're my good daughter. Now you can look like the other little girls. Do you like it, honey?"

Did I like it? I 'bout hugged Mama to death. There was tears in her eyes when she seen how happy I was. And she looked so proud of me as I walked out of the cabin that morning in my fine, new dress. I hadn't never in my whole life had a dress, a real dress. I felt like a queen, and I tried to walk as tall as I could, holding my head high as I got to the classroom. *They'll see me now for sure*, I thought, *because I finally look like the rest of them.*

Two or three girls was standing in a group talking when I come in. One of them stared at me hard, like she was trying to remember something. Then her face smoothed out and she smiled. Smiled at me! She crooked a finger and said, "Mayella, come here a minute, would you?" My heart actually jumped around in my chest as I walked over. She was one of the town girls. Was she going to ask me to play with them at recess? Whatever would I talk about with them? Maybe she was going to say something nice about my dress.

Instead, she said, "Mayella Violet Ewell, whatever are you doing in my old dress? Lord! My mama throwed that out 'cause it wasn't fit to be seen no more."

They all begun to laugh, and I just went hot and cold inside. I felt like throwing up. Then I got mad.

Mad for myself, mad for Mama and all her hard, loving work for me, mad for knowing that I was and always would be a Ewell. I felt like I was falling backwards into a deep, black hole and would never ever get out.

It took two teachers to pull me off that town girl, but not before I'd gotten in some good slaps and bloodied her nose.

Nobody had to tell me I was expelled. I'd already left and was never going back. I walked around downtown till it was my usual time to get home.

Mama met me at the door. "Well, honey, what did they say about your dress? Did they notice it?"

I had to lie. I just couldn't stand having her know what had happened, it would've broke her heart.

"They most positively did, Mama," I said. "Everybody said I looked real pretty, and I thank you, Mama, so much, for my beautiful dress. I'll keep it forever'n'ever."

I took the dress off, folded it carefully, and put it underneath my cot. My old flour sack dress was still hanging on a hook. As I put it on, I felt like I was back in my own skin again, my forever-dirty Ewell skin. I tried to feel ashamed about what I done, losing my temper and fighting, but I realized I couldn't. Actually, I felt myself starting to get tickled about something, and I finally had to laugh out loud.

They sure had noticed Mayella Violet Ewell today, hadn't they?

Chapter 7

The First Loss

My papa wasn't born a drunk and a wife-beater. He wasn't always so spiteful and low-down mean. He didn't used to be hateful of colored people, of Maycomb folks, of his wife and young'uns.

No, in the early days, he was all right. He took a swig or two out of the bottle after supper like most menfolk done. He was good to us, mostly, and worked sometimes. He never had no problem with being so near the colored settlement just down the road.

But as time went on, Papa changed. Life changed him. Sadness and grief that he couldn't or wouldn't speak of, loss of pride and manhood, having to watch his family go without so many things that other folks took for granted—these things changed him. Made him less and less a man, and more and more a drunkard, mad at everybody and everything.

He went from being a husband to Mama to being another child for her to take care of, and needing for her to stand him up just so's he could go out and get falling-down drunk again. He stopped being a father to his young'uns. He was a stranger who often stomped and roared around the cabin. He become someone we feared and tried to keep away from. Spankings turned into whippings, and whippings into beatings.

Papa let life beat him down, then he turned around and beat his family down, beat the colored down. I know what we lost. I know what Papa lost. And I also know that folks lost their lives as a result.

From what Mama told me when I was old enough to hear it, it all begun with the loss of a little life, their first-born son.

*   *   *

Mama was expecting her second child. She and Papa was happy and excited about it, but Papa most specially. He said he felt in his bones that it was going to be a boy, and he wanted the baby to be named after him. Papa loved "his girls," but he wanted a son so bad. That would just cap everything, he thought.

They never had no doctor for any of Mama's birthings. We was too poor. Mama had had me with the help of an old colored midwife—everyone called her Miz Mattie—from the settlement, and Miz Mattie was to help Mama again when her time come.

Problem was, Mama's time come early, way too early.

I don't remember much about that night, just that there was a lot of noise and rushing around. Mama moaning and screaming. Papa sitting with his head in his hands, not saying nothing.

Miz Mattie helped birth that poor child, but he was too young to live and scarcely drawed one breath. After Miz Mattie got Mama cleaned up and quietened, she told Papa the baby might've lived if there'd been a doctor there.

Papa positively blowed up right there and then. He was too proud and stubborn to admit that he couldn't have paid for one, and he must have knowed it was some his fault, what with him not always working steady. But instead of owning up to it and comforting and grieving with Mama, he blamed Miz Mattie. Accused her of the most God-awful things, of letting his son die, all on account of he was a poor man, a poor *white* man, and who did she think she was, setting herself up as so much better'n us and on and on. Said he'd never in his life had any trouble from the colored ('cept he didn't say colored, and I will never write that word), but now she'd better get her black carcass offa his property if she knowed what was good for her. Then he made as if he was going to hit her, but she got to the door first and run off into the night.

And all Mama could do while this was going on was to lay there in bed, weeping, hugging her poor dead baby to her heart.

Papa, still breathing hard, still mad, walked over to where Mama was and looked down on them—his wife and his dead son—and his eyes got mean. He blamed Mama, too, for not giving him a healthy son, and said such hurtful things to her, she never could tell me what they was. If Mama's heart wasn't already broke in two, it was then.

Then Papa took the baby outta her arms and wrapped it in some flour sacking. He went outside and buried the child, Mama never knowed where. Papa kept that secret to hisself.

It was after that night that Papa begun to change. He was a different man forever after, and we couldn't have knowed it right then, but that night, Mama lost her husband, and I lost my papa.

*   *   *

I never heard Miz Mattie's last name till a few years ago. Robinson, Mattie Robinson.

She was *his* grandmother.

Chapter 8

Mama's Good Daughter

It happened to me about two weeks before I turned thirteen. I had woke up in the night not feeling good, like my insides was being pulled apart. My back hurt, too, but I figured that was from all the water I'd hauled the day before for Mama. In the morning when I started to get out of my cot, what I seen near scared me to death.

"Mama! *Mama!*" I screamed. "Mama, help me, I'm bad sick with something, I think I'm dyin'!"

She run over to me and when she seen me, she smiled. A wise and happy smile.

"That ain't nothing to worry about, honey," she comforted me. "You just got your 'time,' is all."

I didn't know what she meant.

"Your monthly time, Mayella. When a girl gets to be about your age, she starts doing this regular, every month. It means she has become a woman. *You* are a woman now, honey."

Papa's voice boomed over us.

"What in the hell are you squallin' about now, Mayella?" Then he seen.

"Jesus Christ, it looks like we butchered a hog in here! Get her cleaned up, Violet. Christ A'mighty, a man don't need to look at that sorta thing before breakfast. It's disgustin'."

"But, Bob, honey, I was just trying to get her calmed down. Mayella's time has done come."

"First of all"—he thunked Mama upside the head—"no sass from you. Second of all, seein' as how you're a 'woman' now, Mayella, you better make sure you keep them legs together from here on out. I ain't havin' no bastard babies in this cabin."

He stomped off to the kitchen, then said over his shoulder, "Keep them legs together, girl, I mean it, or you'll get the strap till you can't stand up no more. You hear me?"

I was crying so hard by now, I couldn't hardly say "Yes, Papa."

Mama held me in her arms and rocked me till I felt better. She got me cleaned and fixed up in the way that women done back then.

After Papa left for the day, she set down with me and explained things, so's I could understand better what had happened to me. She said this should be a happy day for me because besides being a woman now, it meant that someday I could have babies of my own to tend. Then her face got serious.

"Mayella, I want you to listen real close to what I got to say. When the time comes that you start meetin' boys, I want you to promise me, promise me faithful, that you'll only love a good man. Don't pick the very first one, like I—well, never mind."

Her voice trailed off and she sighed. Shook her head slow.

"But—how'll I know if he's good or not, Mama? You said that when you first met Papa, he was real nice and polite."

She set there, thinking of how best to answer me.

Finally she said, "If a man is good on the inside, Mayella, it will show on his outside. I want you to love someone who'll only use his voice to say loving things and only use his hands to hold you close to his heart. I want you to have a man who has kind eyes and gentle ways. And when you find him, he'll love you back, because you have them same things, too."

"I still don't understand how I'll know, Mama."

"When you see him, honey, you'll know right off, I promise you. Your heart will tell you the truth. You will know him right off. That's as good as I can say it."

She stood up.

"But that won't happen for years. So till then, Mayella, maybe you can start making sure that the good that's inside you shows on the outside. And honey, even if you never find that good man, I want you to know that you, you by yourself, are always enough. Always enough. Do you understand better now, child?"

"Yes, I think so, Mama."

"You are my good daughter. My good daughter who is a woman now."

We put our arms around each other, and I never felt closer to her than I done then.

Chapter 9

Mama Becomes Sick

I'm sure Mama was getting sick for a lot longer than we any of us knowed. She never let on, wanting to spare us, the ones she loved, from knowing the worst. Finally she just couldn't hide it no longer.

She'd always had what she called "palpitations"—she'd have to stop what she was doing real sudden and set down for a spell. She said her heart was goin' to beat the band, and I could see it throb on her neck. After it went back to normal, she'd say it wasn't nothing, and get on with her work.

But with every year, it got worse and worse. It got to where's she would sometimes faint, just drop right in her tracks. I'd do what I could for her, rub her wrists, put a cool rag on her face. It always scared me, I was afraid she might not wake up. But she'd get up, and say it was nothing but a weak spell, and not to fret myself about it.

The worst time was when she passed out just as she was putting supper out on the table. Food went everywhere, and there was an awful clatter of broken dishes. This time it was Papa who helped her back to her feet—and then slapped her down again for having made such a mess. Stood over her, too, till she'd cleaned every bit of it up. He finally ordered me to help her, she was moving so slow. I knowed Mama was crying, but didn't want Papa to know. That'd set him off again for sure. At one point, when he wasn't looking, I took her hand and squeezed it. She looked at me, tried to smile and mostly did, and mouthed "Thank you, honey" to me. When you're around somebody all the time, you sometimes don't take notice of things about them. I knowed Mama's "palpitations" was coming at least a couple times a day, but it wasn't till she was taking off her shift one night, that I really seen how thin and little she'd got. I could see all her ribs and backbones. She caught me looking and her face looked like she was grieving over something.

"Mama, you've got to start eatin' more. You're positively skin'n'bones."

She said not to worry, that all womenfolk got skinnier as they got older.

She almost got me believing that.

At first slow and gradual, then quicker as time went on, she got sicker and more wasted. Weaker than she was the day before. It got to where's I could almost see through her.

One evening when Papa chanced to be sober, I made myself get brave and ask him what we should do about Mama. Should she see a doctor? Maybe have an operation?

Papa told me to shut up.

"Ain't nothin' in the world wrong with your ma 'cept plain bone laziness, Mayella. If she keeps this up much longer, she's gonna be one sorry woman."

And then there come the time when Mama couldn't get out of bed no more. Didn't even try. Papa would stand over her, hollering at her to git up, git up *right now*! and fix him his breakfast. It didn't do no good. I think he knowed all along that she was sick, real sick, maybe even dying, and it scared him. Scared him worser than us children already was. He knowed she needed a doctor, but there wasn't no money. No money because he wasn't working, but he for sure had to have his whiskey. So when he hollered and thumped and stomped, it was so's he wouldn't have to know how scared he was, and what a pitiful husband he been.

I had long took over doing most of the chores around the cabin. Mama was sleeping more and more, but when she was awake, she wanted all her young'uns around her. It was enough for her just to be able to reach out and hold onto one of her babies. She wanted her geraniums, too, put where she could see them all the time. I tried to make things as nice as I could for her. When I was busy doing things for her, it kept me from thinking and being afraid.

Then when she'd fell back asleep, all of us would be quiet as mice. Sometimes us children would just set around in a clump on the dirt floor of our cabin, not talking, not moving, almost not breathing. Just setting there like we was all waiting for something to happen.

And we was. We just didn't know how bad things would be when it finally come.

Chapter 10

The Second Loss

No matter how many years have passed, I still have the same dream about when Mama died. Only it's not like a real dream, where funny or unbelievable things happen, and when you wake up, none of it was real or true. No. When I dream of Mama, it's the way it really happened, and when I wake, it's still real, still true.

Mama's calling me.

As I walk over to her bed, I ache to see how thin and wasted she's gotten. In some places, her bones seem near to coming through her skin. Her dark eyes, still beautiful in spite of her pain, are enormous in her tired face. She's putting all her love for me in her eyes as she looks up at me. She tries to smile, and says she's not afraid, that she's ready, but I am afraid, and I'm not ready. What'll I do when she's gone? Who'll keep us safe from Papa when he's been drinking? Who will ever again touch me with gentle hands and loving looks?

She can only whisper now.

Come here, honey, set with me a bit. No, you won't hurt me none, come closer. Take my hand, that's right. Hold it tight, and don't let go.

You always was my good daughter. You always will be.

I'm so grieved to leave y'all like this, Mayella. I'm so sorry to be putting all the care of the children, and Papa, and the cabin on you. I wisht it didn't have to be so, but I can't help it.

If you ever get afraid, honey, I want you to remember what I'm sayin' now.

You got grit, Mayella, deep down inside you. You don't know how much yet, but it's there, I know it's there.

If anyone starts to fret you, promise me you'll show 'em what you're made of. Spit in their eye if you have to. Let 'em know you ain't called upon to take no disrespect from anybody.

And Mayella, if your paw, or any of your brothers ever start to—bother you or your sisters, you just gotta stand right up to 'em. Make 'em know you ain't afraid. They will see how strong you are. A beatin's easier to take than—the other thing.

Keep the family together as best you can, honey. I know you'll always do what's right.

I'll be watching over you from whatever place in Heaven the Lord sees fit to give me. Don't never forget that. You won't be able to see me no more, but you'll know I'm always, always with you. You won't be alone, child. Ever.

I keep hold of her hand, and hers in mine gets weaker and weaker. I almost can't tell when she stops breathing, her passing is so gentle.

"Mama? Mama! Ma—"

But I know she has left me, left me forever.

I lay my head on the pillow next to hers. I feel a little breeze brush my cheek. It's more'n likely the wind coming in, but I have to believe, I must believe, that it's her dear soul leaving. Leaving her body, leaving us, leaving her home. But not without one last caress, to tell me that all is well with her at last.

Chapter 11

Family Forever

I kept her hand in mine under the blanket for I don't know how long after she passed. It was still so warm—was she giving me the last little bit of her warmth, or was I trying to keep hers from leaving? Maybe if I never let go, she wouldn't really be dead.

I couldn't speak, couldn't cry, couldn't scream. Couldn't hardly think what to do now. Just kept kneeling there by her, holding her hand. It was so still in the cabin, I nearly forgot about the children being there. There was only me and Mama. I tried to pray. Mama would have knowed what to pray, I didn't. My mind was running crazy away from me. *She's gone, dead, dead, always and forever, I won't see her no more in this life. Who'll love me now? Laugh with me? Who's gonna take care of me and my brothers and sisters and keep us safe from when Papa's been drinking? God, I'm trying to pray to you, but I don't understand, how can you take her from me like this, right now, when I need her so bad? All I ever wanted was someone of my own to love, and love me back. Did you need her more, God? I want to believe that she's with you, no pain now, no more sadness, with you in Heaven and watching over me. But I'm sorry, God, I just want her back. Please be nice to her, and let her be happy in Heaven, she's had such an awful time here with Papa. Maybe you'll let her come back to me sometimes? Even if I can't see her, I'll know she's near, I'll feel her there. I know I will.*

There was a little sound next to me and I looked up. There stood Burris, the others was hanging back aways. "Is Mama dead, Mayella?" he asked. He tried to make his voice like Papa's, rough and deep, but I could see his eyes was filling with tears.

"Yes, honey, she's passed. She's went to a better place now," I said.

He ducked his head down and mumbled something I couldn't make out. Now the children was coming over, looking at Mama, not understanding, some of them crying, some of them just staring. They started pelting me with questions. *What's dead mean, Mayella? Will Papa die too? When's supper? Why's her eyes still open? Will she be better tomorrow?* I couldn't begin to even get my mind around the things they was asking. I felt dizzy, like I might faint. I loosed Mama's hand real quick and stood up, wild to run out of the cabin, run anywhere, just so's I could be free of that room so full of loss and fear and sadness.

I was most out the door when I gasped—I swear I heard Mama's voice in my head. Spoke just as natural as if she was standing right by me, sounding more alive than she'd ever been. I closed my eyes and listened, then I knowed just what to do.

I went back to where Mama lay and told the children to all hush a minute. I made all eight of us to stand in a little half circle around her. I took hold of Mama's hand again, and told Burris to go on the other side and hold her other hand. Then I took a deep breath and told the others to take each other's hand. Finally we made one solid chain around our Mama, with her at the top, holding us together in that one moment, just like she always done in life.

"Keep tight to each other," I said. I made my voice sound fierce, like I was mad, because I could feel the tears wanting to come. "This is the way it's always been, and will be forever. We'll always be linked together like this, no matter what. *Because we're family.* Mama wants us to know this, know it down to our hearts. Down to our souls. We will always and forever be family."

Such a sweet peace come as we stood over her, loving her with our eyes, thanking her, saying goodbye. I felt a great pain in my chest for a moment before we all let go, and I knowed it was part of Mama's soul coming into my heart. I haven't had many holy moments in my life, but this one, I knowed, would be with me forever.

Chapter 12

Learning to Hate

But that beautiful quiet couldn't last. I knowed it wouldn't. I heard Papa coming long before I seen him. His boot heels stomping against the makeshift boards of the porch. Singing a song, off-key, at the top of his lungs, a bad song, not fitting for the children to hear. He must have took a tumble because I heard his hands smack hard against the step. Then the cussing—up one side and down the other. I didn't have to smell him, neither, to know he was drunk outta his mind. He always was, most days.

The door banged open, most come off its hinges, and he stood there on the doorstep, swaying, trying to take it all in, all of us still around Mama's bed. The rotten smell of moonshine whiskey hit me like the back of his hand. He blinked his eyes hard a couple of times, getting used to the dark of the cabin. Seems like he stood there an hour, and I was fearful of what he might say or do to us.

Finally he seen me, then looked at the still, frail body in the bed.

"What's wrong with y'all? What're y'all standin' around here for?"

Then he looked closer at Mama.

"Is she . . . is she dead now, Mayella?"

I could only nod.

"How long?"

"I dunno. Not long, Papa."

He looked at Mama again, then his face begun to sag like it had no muscles to hold it up. It finally sunk into his brain that she had really passed, and then he like to give me a mortal scare by letting out a God-awful howl that ended in a low moan. He begun to cry, cry in that sloppy, messy way that drunk men do.

"Aw, Violet, my sweet l'il Violet," he groaned as he staggered across the cabin to the bed. "You ain't really dead, now, are ya? Mayella, tell me she ain't really dead. C'mon, Violet, git up! Please honey!"

It made me sick to hear him, and I told the children to run outside for a bit.

His voice suddenly turned mean.

"Git up now, woman. I mean it, git up, Goddam you, or by God, I'll give you the strap till you can't stand up no more!"

Then he was back to sobbing and snuffling again, mumbling, "Please, honey, c'mon Violet, it just can't be so!"

He suddenly went sprawling, right across her poor body.

"How'm I sposed to take care of all these brats now, Violet? Huh? *Answer me, you worthless slut!* You made'em, now I'm gonna have to look after'em all 'cause you was always a selfish bit—"

I had to stop him.

"She's dead, Papa. She can't hear you no more."

I tried to make my voice deep so's he'd listen. I helped him get off the bed and layed out on the floor. He stopped crying long enough to be sick on hisself. It nearly made me do it too, to smell it. I went to get a rag to clean him up some, but by the time I come back, he had passed out, his hiccups and snuffling and cussing getting less and less until it was quiet once more in the cabin.

As I looked down on him, I felt mad enough—I hated him enough—to kill him right then and there. I could've done it easy, too, I would just get a knife from the kitchen, or maybe the dump.

I shook myself all over. I just couldn't let myself think that way. Mama would be ashamed of me. I set my jaw so hard it hurt, and promised her to not feel so mad, to not hate so much, but Lord, it was hard. I thought of all the times I'd seen her hit, shoved, beat with the belt, drug around by her hair, her beautiful hair. Thought of all the bruises and swelled-up eyes and welts he'd give her. Once even a broke arm.

My tears started coming, but I clenched my fists and made them go back. I thought, *You never loved her, did you, Papa? Or any of us. You don't deserve to have knowed her, don't deserve to grieve for her now. You ain't worth nothin', Papa. Nothin'.*

I felt very far away from Mama now as I watched Papa laying there on the floor, stinking of liquor, twitching and belching and passing wind. And that was when I come to know, knowed down to my very heart and soul, that I was gonna have to grow up awful fast now. I had a family to look after, to take care of. They would all need me now. And I prayed to God and Mama that I would be able to do everything for them that she would have done, and that maybe sometimes she would look down on me from her Heaven and be proud of me and still call me her good daughter.

My legs couldn't hold me up no more, so I sunk onto the dirt floor by Mama's cot, being real careful not to touch nor rouse Papa. I closed my eyes and wanted so much to just go to sleep, sleep forever, and never wake up. I was tired, I'd never been so tired, and it felt good to lay there for a little bit with my eyes closed, just for a few minutes.

Chapter 13

The Third Loss

"Git up, you worthless slut! Git up, Mayella, you ain't gonna lay in bed half the day. You clean up this place, it looks like a pigsty, and I want my breakfast. It better be on the table when I get back, or you'll get the back of my hand." Papa stomped off and slammed the door to the cabin.

His words had went through me like a knife. I hadn't been sleeping, just laying there and thinking of what all I had to do today, and wondering if there would be enough food for the children, and how I could keep Papa from whipping them. No matter how old they was, I still thought of my brothers and sisters as "the children," and had took over Mama's place since she had passed in protecting them from our paw.

I raised myself up a little ways and gasped. My back still wasn't right since the night he'd throwed me up against the wall for breaking a dish. How long had it been paining me? I tried to think. A week? Ten days? It was getting harder and harder for me to keep track of time these days. Here it was, most a year since Mama had died, and her passing was still a raw, ragged place in my heart.

I crawled slow and careful out of my cot, and rubbed the sore places on my back till it got so's I could stand all the way up. I didn't need to dress myself. I always slept with my clothes on now, even on the hottest nights. I'd made my sisters do the same. I never knowed when Papa might come home late some night, full of moonshine and evil thoughts. The first time it happened to me, I was lucky. He was so drunk that I just pushed him onto the floor and rolled him to the fartherest corner of the cabin. He never knowed a thing.

I went into the kitchen to start putting out breakfast. If Papa come back before I was done, there'd be hell to pay and a strap across the back of my legs.

Breakfast was always the same thing. I reached down the cracked plate of cold biscuit, and begun to warm last night's gravy. Sometimes we had a little meat, but Papa hadn't went hunting in a while. I put out our mismatched plates and saucers, retrieved from the dump over the years, then scooted some wooden crates and boxes up to the table so we most of us could set. I done it this way every morning, ever since Mama had died, and I reckoned I could do it in my sleep. There, everything was pretty near ready, I could start getting the children up now. *The children.* Oh God, how could I forget?

I looked down at the table and yes, I'd set it as nice as I could, as nice as Mama always done. But I'd gone and set out too many plates. There wasn't as many of us now as before. I set down on a crate and thought about the day I lost four of my brothers and sisters—Luther, Garnet, and the twins Amelia and Miranda—all at once.

It had happened right after Mama's death. Things was in a mess. I didn't know the proper things to do when a family member passed, but I knowed I couldn't count on Papa to be of any help. I finally decided to walk to town and call some of Mama's people. They would help me, they would know what to do. We hadn't seen nor heard much from them for quite a long spell. None of them had ever took to Papa very much. But I knowed in my heart that her family would want the burying of her. I talked to one of her sisters, my aunt Pansy, and she promised to come out the next day. I felt relieved to know that all the right things would be done for Mama, and that she could rest near to her folks.

True to her word, Aunt Pansy and her husband drove in the very next morning. They was most strangers to me, but they greeted me kindly and said they was sorry for my loss, then asked if Papa was around. I was glad he wasn't. Probably off in the woods seeing to his still. He'd never really sobered up good the last few days.

I took them inside, and I could see in their faces and their eyes how shocked they was at how the cabin looked, how the dump smelled, how we lived in dirt. It shamed me for them to see.

My aunt looked so much like Mama, the very moral of her, and I couldn't hardly take my eyes off her. It was like water to a thirsty man. Some of the children was inside, but they was shy of strangers and stayed aways off. Aunt Pansy took my hand, and we walked to where Mama still lay in bed. We both of us kneeled down beside her. She looked at Mama's face for the longest time. I seen tears coming in her eyes, her lips trembled, and she took some raggedy, hitching breaths. Finally she leaned down to Mama, kissed her forehead and eyes, and whispered to her. I caught some of the words, like "my poor dear sister" and "God keep you always" and "we'll see to you now." Then after one little sob, she straightened her shoulders and stood up. She nodded to her husband—I understood he would get Mama's body ready to move—then she took me outside, into the sunshine. She said a power of lovely things, comforting words, pressing my hand like she cared about me. She said I wasn't to worry about nothing, Mama would be took care of and layed next to Grandma and Grandpa. When I heard that, I was so happy, I begun to cry. Then suddenly she took me in her arms, just like Mama would've done, and she hugged me close to her. Her voice sounded so like Mama's, that I pretended for a few moments that it was really my mama, come back to life, come back to me, to hold me and love me and comfort me.

Quiet and gentle, Aunt Pansy begun asking me questions about my brothers and sisters, their ages, their names, did we have enough to eat, was our paw good to us, and so on. I answered her truly about the children, but fibbed about the other things. What good would it do to tell the truth now?

She was just starting to tell me some stories about when her and Mama was little, when my uncle come out with Mama's body wrapped in a comforter they'd brung with them. He carried her real careful as if she'd been a fragile piece of glass and layed her in the car. From off in the distance, I could see Papa coming. He didn't look too far gone, thank goodness. My aunt and uncle looked at each other again and asked me to go back inside the cabin, and said that they had something particular they wanted to discuss with him.

Our cabin had no windows to speak of, so I heard everything. They offered, in the nicest and kindest way, to take the two youngest children, the twins, back with them to raise. It'd be a saving to him, they said, and to our family, there'd be fewer mouths to feed, less work for me, and they felt like it'd be honoring Mama to do it. Papa reeled back a little—more likely from liquor than surprise—and commenced to hollering. Who were they to tell him how to take care of his family, a poor widow-man like him? He was the most God-fearin', hardest-workin' man in these parts, and a good provider and a good husband, and he seen to his children, by God . . .

His words was all slurry, but finally he run out of things to say.

Then to my complete shock, his next words was, well, as long as they was wanting two, why not take four? It was all the same to him, he said. No one spoke for a minute. I couldn't hardly get my breath. I knowed all too well that Papa never took no notice if any of us was sick, or hungry, or hurt. But I never thought I'd see any man, even a man like my papa, so low-down that he'd give away his children like they was just so many mongrel pups from too large a litter.

Well, it ended with my aunt and uncle asking me to get the four youngest ones ready to leave with them. The poor babies, they didn't understand why they was to go away from their family, or who they was going with, but I told them that they was going to have some real good times now. They'd get to live in a house, a real house, with their own rooms. They'd get schooled proper, have all they wanted to eat, and never have to wear clothes made from feedsacks again. There'd be no more bad smells, no more dirt and ugliness, no more beatings. And they could all go visit Mama's grave whenever they wanted.

Papa didn't even say goodbye to his children. I tried to hold all four of'em in my arms at once, and I kissed them, and told them never to forget that we was all Mama's children, always and forever. My aunt and uncle kissed me and hugged me goodbye, and promised to write and let me know how they all was doing. They promised they would treat the young'uns like they was their own, and told me to hold on and have faith.

As they was getting into the car, I grabbed up a pot of Mama's geraniums and asked Aunt Pansy to please put them on her grave. Mama would like that, and I felt a little better knowing that she'd have her beloved flowers near her. I also knowed without even asking that Papa wasn't gonna let none of the rest of us be at Mama's burying. So all's I could do was hope—no, I had to believe—that if Mama's soul was ever to look down and see her geraniums, she'd know that we was there in spirit. And that brung me some comfort.

So at last I stood on the porch, watching and waving as long as I could, till I couldn't see them no more.

At that moment, I lost my Mama all over again, and four of my brothers and sisters. I knowed Mama would rest easy now that she was near her people and that she'd have perfect peace at last. And I knowed the children would have better and happier lives than I ever would.

And at that moment, I wasn't sure who I envied more.

Chapter 14

Chopping Kindling

Every day was exactly the same as the day before. Though I had used to help Mama with the chores, I'd never realized how much hard work she actually done all by herself, and how much of her day went into trying to keep our cabin nice for us.

Such a power of work I and my sister Sally had to do now! Cooking, washing up, mending, hauling water several times a day, picking through the dump in hopes of finding something useful, trying to keep the dirt floor of the cabin swept. Sally wasn't near as strong as me, so she couldn't help me much with the real heavy work. I got up in the dark and I went to bed when it had got dark again. I felt like an old woman, wore out and bent over with never-ending work, never-ending grief and worry.

I didn't hardly have a minute during the day to think of the four youngest children who had been took for raising by Aunt Pansy. I had a letter or two from her to say that they was all of them doing real well, and was getting their schooling. I missed them, I missed my mama, but I could only let myself cry for them at night when I was in my cot.

My two brothers who'd stayed here—Burris and Elias— tried to help some around the cabin. But they was boys, and would rather go around with their paw, or just be off in the woods by theirselves. Sometimes I could talk them into hauling me in an extra bucket of water, moving something big to or from the dump, or chopping kindling for me. While I worked, I thought back to the many times Mama had stepped in between Papa's strap and us children, to take the beating herself. That had become my job now too.

The only thing that never felt like work was when I was tending to Mama's geraniums. I didn't have no proper pots for them, just some slop jars I got from the dump. I took care to keep them watered just right, pinched the dead leaves off, and rooted new ones. It was like part of Mama was still alive in those plants, and I was taking care of her by taking care of them. I could almost feel her soul coming into me through the leaves and flowers when I touched them. She was right—geraniums was for comfort, and it was the only happy part of my day. Those moments was like heaven to me.

I don't know exactly when it was that I begun to feel—sorta empty inside. It was like something was missing or left out of me. I felt alone, all alone, and that was funny, because with seven brothers and sisters, I'd probably never been alone a day in my whole life. And now when there was just the five of us, and I was sitting in the midst of my family, that was when I felt the loneliest.

I knowed I needed something I didn't have, I just didn't know what it was.

Then one night after I'd went to bed, it come to me—I wished I had a friend. I'd never really had one before. Sally was all right, but she was my sister and it just wasn't the same thing. I thought about how fine and nice it would be to talk to someone, someone outside of this cabin, this family. I could tell them my secrets, my hopes, my sorrows. I would know theirs.

How would I get a friend? How would I be one?

I never hardly had any time to go into town and see folks. I couldn't visit in the settlement down the road from us, Papa'd take my head off. Or worse.

So I guessed a friend would have to come to me.

I shook my head at myself. *Mayella Violet Ewell*, I thought, *just who do you think is gonna come here to be* your *special friend?* It was stupid, stupid and foolish to think of such a thing. Like Papa would sometimes say: "Wish in one hand, and spit in the other, and see which one gets full first."

But then Mama's voice come into my head. She'd often tell me, "Just take it to the Lord in prayer, Mayella. He'll always listen." That was from her favorite hymn. I remembered another part of it: "Can we find a friend so faithful, who will all our sorrows share?"

Well, maybe God could send me a friend. I thought it wouldn't hurt none to pray on it, and so I did till I fell asleep.

*   *   *

It was maybe a week after that. The morning had started out pretty bad. Papa had "overslept" himself, as he put it—*for what?* I always wondered to myself—and was feeling cantankerous.

"Biscuits is tough again, Mayella. Ain't you ever gonna learn to cook right?"

"I'm sorry, Papa. I try to make them just like Mama's."

He reached over and fetched me a slap on my cheek.

"Don't you never mention that worthless slut in front of me again, girl, not in this house. It was her what deserted me and left me with all you damn brats to feed. And a hard time I have of it, too. You should be grateful to your paw for everything I'm doing for y'all. You make them biscuits better tomorrow, Mayella, or you'll be sorry."

He finished eating, belched real loud and stood up.

"You're gettin' to be more and more like your slut of a ma, Mayella."

He walked to the door and turned. Looked up and down my body real slow and a little grin danced in his eyes.

"And you look like her too. A lot like her."

I thought he'd went, but he stuck his head back in the door.

"And make sure you get some kindling busted up today. We're most out. There's a couple bureau drawers in the dump you can use. Bust 'em up good. And clean up this rat's nest of a cabin, how do you expect a hard-workin' man like me to make a honest livin' in a mess like this?"

He grunted and stomped off.

I sighed. Papa knowed how much I hated chopping kindling. It was the ax—it was real heavy, and my arms wasn't any too strong. The first time I'd tried to do it, I'd near cut my own foot off.

Burris and Elias had already went off, and Sally was out fetching some water, so I'd have to do it myself. Well, I'd do it first thing, so's to get it out of the way.

I got the drawers out of the dump and layed one on the stump I used for chopping. Saying a prayer, I raised the ax over my head—and somehow my feet got all tangled up and I lost my balance. I just went over backwards—right onto my backside. I sat there for a minute, not knowing whether I should laugh or cry. But before I could raise myself off the dirt, there was a gentle voice that come from above me, from the road in front of our cabin.

"'Scuse me, ma'am, but c'n I give you a hand with that?"

PART 2

Chapter 15

A Friend

"Ain't this the second time this week you done washed your hair, Mayella?"

I raised my dripping head from the bucket and wrenched out as much water as I could.

Sally was standing over me, looking like she thought I musta lost my mind.

"Well, and so what if it is? T'ain't none of your business, and 'sides, *your* head could do with a washing, too, miss. Why don't you go fetch another bucket of water and . . ."

That was enough to send my sister running out the door. Good. I wanted to be alone for a spell.

I went out on the porch and begun to comb out my hair so's it could dry in the sun. *All right*, I thought, *I have been trying to keep myself cleaner lately. After all, I was most nineteen, a young lady now, and Mama always said that you could tell a lady by her—*

Well, just stop it, Mayella Violet Ewell, I scolded myself. *Tell the truth and shame the devil, like the preacher says. You know good and well why you been keepin' yourself fixed up these last few weeks.* And I did, too. It started sometime after I'd met Tom Robinson and he'd helped me bust up all that kindling.

There I had been, flat on my backside on the ground, and knowing that if I couldn't do this chore, Papa'd skin me alive.

And there *he* had been, passing by on his way to the fields or somewheres. He'd asked if he could help me.

When I got up and seen it was a colored man, I felt a shock go through me, and I backed up a little closer to the cabin.

"Oh, no," I said, "I can handle it, thank you anyways."

And I went to lift up the ax again.

"I don't mean no disrespec', ma'am, but that's a mighty big ax for you to be messin' with. I'm 'fraid you might hurt yo'self."

That was when I looked closer at his face, into his eyes. Those eyes was kind, and he looked like he didn't mean me no harm. I didn't know what to do. I was biting the inside of my cheek and thinking. I hadn't heard a kind word from anybody since—well, since Aunt Pansy had come after Mama died. That was an awful long time ago.

He stood there a little longer, then raised his cap and said, "Well, mornin' to you, ma'am." He started to walk away.

I decided.

"Wait," I said. "I reckon it wouldn't hurt nothin' if you was to help. That's, that's right kindly of you."

He come into the yard—yes, I had let a Negro onto our property. If anybody had seen!

He hefted up the ax, and that's when I saw his arm—or what was left of it. I stopped him. "But how c'n you—with your arm and all—?" I didn't know how to say it, and didn't want to seem rude.

"That's all right, ma'am, I've learned real well how to get along of it just fine. It won't be no trouble. Now, please, ma'am, just could you maybe stand off aways, so's I don't hit you with no chips."

And he went to work. He was real strong, and it didn't seem like no time at all till there was a good-sized pile of kindling by the stump.

He layed the ax down, and begun to walk towards the road.

I'd been quiet while he worked, but then I suddenly remembered the manners Mama had taught me.

"Thank you. Thank you, Mr—uh?"

"Robinson, ma'am. Tom Robinson. I lives just down the road."

"Well, I thank you again for helpin' me, Mr. Robinson. Wait, let me just go in the house and see can I give you a nickel or—"

"Ain't no need to pay me, ma'am. I'se just glad I could help. Thank you, ma'am."

He raised his cap to me again and went along his way.

Chapter 16

Learning to Love Again

As I watched him walk down the road, I thought, *He thanked me.* He *thanked* me. I just couldn't get over it. The only time anymore I heard them words was when Papa'd holler, "I'll thank you to shut your stupid mouth, slut." And him calling me "ma'am." Nobody'd *never* called me that in my life!

After the first time that Tom helped me, it seemed that little by little, I begun to watch for him to walk by outside mornings and evenings. Sometimes if I knowed I was alone, I'd wave to him from the porch. He most always would ask could he do anything for me. He seemed to be so friendly, like I could trust him, that I did start letting him help me with a chore now and then. And I kept offering to pay him, but he always said no, there wasn't no need, he had to pass by this way anyways. After a time, I didn't offer no more.

Then it got so's I'd try to think up chores that he could do, because I'd got into a way of talking to him while he worked.

It felt so good to have someone to talk to, someone not from my family. Sometimes I'd talk so much, it was like I was trying to get everything out I had stored up inside me over the years. I talked about my grandparents, and how my mama had got sick and died. I told him about the beautiful dress she had done made over for me. About her geraniums that I was now watching over for her. How I was working so hard to take care of what was left of my family and trying to keep my brothers in school. I didn't know I had so much to say, but Tom was a good listener and didn't seem to mind. Couple times, I started to tell about Papa and all his carrying-on, but I never did, I was so ashamed for anybody to know. Tom knowed my name was Ewell, but that didn't seem to matter none to him.

One morning as I was clearing up after breakfast, it suddenly come to me. I had a friend! Just like I'd prayed for. Tom Robinson was my friend, and I never in this world woulda thought that I'd have a colored man for a friend.

And I also never thought that I would fall in love with him too.

I don't know how it happened, or when. I just knowed I felt happy when he was here, and lonely when he was not. He had such gentle ways. I could tell by his eyes that there wasn't a spiteful bone in his body. Mama had once told me—I had never forgot—about how a man had to be the same outside as he was inside. Tom wasn't loud and hateful like Papa. I never smelled liquor on him. He spoke so proud of his family and his young'uns that I knowed they was never beaten. He kept hisself clean and worked steady all the time.

He was the kindest person I'd knowed since I lost Mama. How could I *not* have loved him?

I knowed it would never come to nothing. There wasn't no way it could have. I wouldn't have wanted it to. Tom was married and I could tell, the way he spoke and acted, that he never felt more'n a friend to me. But that was all right. That was enough for me. I'd never loved a man before, and it made me feel wonderful and special inside, like I had something to live for. Like I had a precious secret that only I knowed about.

But I also knowed how dangerous it was for me to even have had him come inside our fence. Papa positively hated Negroes, had ever since the time his son had died being born. He always said the most ugliest things about them, and told

me time after time what he would do to me if he ever seen
me talking to one.

But Mama, when she was still alive, had felt different.
She didn't let on to Papa, of course, that would have meant a
beating. But sometimes after Papa had been on a tear about
our neighbors in the settlement, she'd take me aside afterwards
and tell me that we all of us was God's children, and that He
didn't care a whit about the color of our skin, He loved us all
just the same. We was just all human beings, she said, trying
to get through life best as we could, and that we should
always, always be kind and gentle to each other.

I believed the exact way as Mama done, but I was very
careful to make sure that Papa was nowheres around when it
come time for Tom to pass by. I didn't think none of the
children would tattle on me, but I wasn't completely sure—if
Burris and Elias wasn't in school, sometimes they'd be in the
cabin whenever Tom was there. So I took them and Sally
aside one night when Papa was out, and told them there wasn't
nothing wrong with Tom helping me out, that was what
neighbors did, and that colored folks wasn't no different from
us and could be our friends. And if they didn't tell Papa, I
promised them I'd take them to town for ice creams real soon.
They didn't get ice cream hardly ever, and this really seemed
to tickle them, so I thought I didn't need to fret about them
telling on me.

But it was actually me, in a way, that caused Papa to finally
find out.

One evening as I was starting to fix supper, Burris, who
was standing at the window, called over to me, "Hey, Mayella,
here comes your nig—." But before he could finish, I had ran
over to him and slapped him. Hard. He looked shocked, then
he got mad as a hornet, that I could do such a thing to him,
and truth to tell, I was shocked at myself. I'd never took a
hand to any of my brothers and sisters.

"Don't you never, ever let me hear you say that again,
Burris Ewell!"

I wanted to shake him.

"Papa says it all the time," he yelled. "I'm a man like Papa now, and you ain't got no right to tell me what to do!"

"Burris," I said, "you don't want to be like Papa. You don't want to say things like that. It's wrong. Mama wouldn't never have—"

Burris made like he was gonna hit me back, but only sassed me.

"I'll say whatever I wanta say, Mayella Ewell, and there ain't nothin' you c'n do about it. I'm a man now!" Then he made an ugly face at me, and run out of the cabin.

In the end, it hurt me, but I wasn't really surprised when I found out it was Burris had told Papa.

Chapter 17

Betrayal

The things that happened next, I'm so ashamed of, I can't hardly write of them. But I have promised to tell the truth, and I will, for the memory of the ones I loved who are in Heaven now. I'm ready to tell the truth about what really happened the day Papa seen me and Tom in the cabin together.

Papa come in drunk the night before, and tried to—well, I can't say it no other way—he got into bed with me. I couldn't hardly fight him off this time. He got me so's I was pinned down and couldn't kick or nothing. And then he—but I won't go on about what happened after that, because some things is too just evil to be spoke of.

The next morning when I woke up, Papa was gone. I couldn't hardly move, what with him twisting my arms and back so the night before. Inside, I felt numb and in shock about what Papa'd did to me.

As the children and I ate breakfast, I could tell Burris was still mad at me for slapping him. Wouldn't look at me, nor talk to me. I told him I was sorry about what I done to him, but that the words he'd been saying was bad and sinful. It wasn't no use, though. He got up and stomped out the door, just like Papa. It was sometime later that day that he told Papa about me and Tom.

When I invited Tom into the cabin that afternoon, I didn't know things would fall apart so quick. I can't explain why I done or said them things I did. Maybe because I was mad at Papa for what he done to me the night before. I felt soiled and shamed of being a woman, of having a woman's body that could be used so cruel by my own paw. I just wanted—I just wanted a little comfort from Tom, because he was my friend, and that's what friends do. I wanted him to hold me like my mama used to and tell me everything would be all right. And I guess I *did* want him to kiss me, so's it would maybe wipe away a little of what Papa done to me.

So when Tom turned away from me and went to leave, I felt it was because I must be so dirty that no one wouldn't never want to touch me, nor even be my friend. That's when I got upset and said all them terrible things to him. Tried to *make* him kiss me. I scared him for sure—who wouldn't'a been scared of me? I was like a wild woman, I wasn't thinking clear, and I was even scaring myself. All I knowed was that I hated my life, the filth, the drunkenness, being told I was a worthless slut and then treated like one. I'd had enough of being a Ewell.

Tom Robinson was a man who'd never been nothing but kind and respectful to me. He was the first person who ever called me "ma'am." He was my friend, the first and only one I'd ever had. Though it was wrong, I loved him. If he didn't want me, who would?

And yet, I done them things to him, and said them awful words, and it was right in the middle of all that ruckus, that Papa come busting into the cabin.

Thank God, Tom got away before Papa could kill him.

But me—Papa proceeded to lay into me like he never done before. Used his fists, used the strap, used a piece of firewood. If I hadn't'a passed out when I did, I know he woulda killed me. Next thing I knowed, the sheriff was there, firing question after question at me. Papa was hollering in the background, and he wouldn't shut up. My head was spinning,

I felt sick, and I just wanted the noise to stop. Wanted everybody to go away and leave me be. Wanted Papa not to hit me again. Finally, I couldn't take it no more and so I told them what they wanted to hear. *Yes*, I said, *I was raped. Yes, I was beat up. Yes, yes, yes, only please stop talking.*

And then later when the sheriff brung Tom before me, I again said, *Yes. Yes, that's him.*

*   *   *

I healed up from my bruises and my blacked eyes. I healed up from the rape. But I won't never heal up from having give Tom up to Papa, to the sheriff, to the law. And I will never heal up from knowing that I as good as killed Tom Robinson that afternoon in the cabin.

Chapter 18

Lies

Tom's case come to trial several months later.

The disgraceful way Papa and me acted, and the low-down, black lies we told in court has already been wrote on the public record, and I can't hardly bear to tell it again here. Whenever I remember it, I always hope it'll have a different ending, but I know that can't never happen.

The only thing I got to say about it now is, I *was* raped and I *was* beat up, but not by Tom Robinson. And how Mr. Finch knowed this, and who really done it, I still don't understand.

I wonder what Mama thought of me as she watched from Heaven and saw me lie and accuse and betray such a good and innocent man. I'm sure she wouldn't'a knowed it was me, the one she always called her "good daughter."

When she was dying, she told me that I had grit and that I shouldn't let nobody see when I'm afraid. Spit in their eye, she said, and don't take no disrespect.

The way I acted to Mr. Finch, the judge, and everybody else that day—I told myself I was just doing what Mama had told me to do. But what I was really doing was being more afraid of another beating—or worse—from Papa than of telling the truth.

Mama had also told me that the color of our skin don't matter, and that we must all be kind and gentle with everyone, because God loves us all the same.

With the lies I told, I failed her, dishonored her memory, and shamed myself to my very soul forever.

I am so sorry for what I done that day in court. I shoulda spoke up and said what really happened. Mr. Finch give me every chance to, but I was mortally afraid. He didn't have to go home with Papa at the end of the day like I did. The saving of a good man's life shoulda meant more to me than a beating.

Tom was found guilty, of course, and sent to prison. Guilty. Yes, he was guilty—guilty of being kind to a poor white trash girl, a Ewell, of treating her with respect, and of being the best and only friend she ever had. Tom Robinson had taught me what it was to love someone better than yourself, enough to want to give your life for them.

Well—a life was given, all right. But it was the wrong one. *It shoulda been mine.*

Chapter 19

Broken Flowers

It was over.

Papa walked ahead of me as we left the courtroom. Well, he didn't so much walk as strut. Held his head high like he was proud of hisself and dared anybody to say otherwise. That was 'bout the longest walk I ever took. I knowed everybody wanted to get a good look at me, so I ducked my head down. I didn't have to see their faces to know what they thought about the Ewells that day.

We was most out the door when everything hit me all at once. I pushed Papa out of the way so's I could get outside and behind the bushes, where I got sick. I thought I would never stop. I think I was trying to sick up my lies and my disgrace. Sick up being who I was and what I done to a innocent man.

Papa hollered at me to come on. He hated to watch folks being sick—said it was downright humiliating to see me do something like that in public, and I'd best stop if I knowed what was good for me. If he only realized how many times I'd had to clean him up when he was drunk. 'Course, he wouldn't know that because he was usually passed out cold at the time.

I got myself stopped, and as I walked home, my stomach settled down some. Then as we got in sight of our cabin, I could see something on the porch. Couldn't tell exactly, but it looked like splotches of red, bright red, bright scarlet. Maybe one of the children had hurt theirselves and it was blood! I run the rest of the way, and when I seen what it really was, I wanted to be sick all over again.

Someone had kicked over all the slop jars that Mama's geraniums had been in. They'd busted the jars to bits, but worst of all was they had tromped all over the plants and mashed them into the dirt. Red petals was scattered everywhere, like drops of blood for sure.

I cried as I gathered as many of the broke plants as I could and put them in my lap. The jars I didn't pay no mind to. But my mama's geraniums—the ones she'd set so much store by, that she'd passed on to me to take care of—how could somebody have took something so beautiful and fragile and crushed the life outta them? What kind of person was this? Them flowers wasn't hurting nobody, all they asked for was some sun and water, a little loving attention, and they would give back only beauty and comfort.

I set on the porch grieving over Mama's flowers like they was so many little dead babies. Papa finally hauled up and looked at the mess. Grunted. Then said, "Clean this up, Mayella, then go start my supper. Showin' up those high-toned gents in court today has give me a right good appetite tonight." He stomped off towards the woods.

I looked down at what was left of the flowers and seen that some of them still had their roots. I hoped, I prayed, that there was enough of them for me to try to bring them back to life. I sorted through them and found a good many that I might could save.

Mama's geraniums wasn't totally lost. I did manage to get most of them rooted and growing again.

I never found out who done it, but I never forgot the message they was trying to tell me with them busted pots and crushed flowers:

What that person done to the geraniums, I done the same thing that day in court to Tom Robinson.

Chapter 20

The Fourth Loss

After the trial, my life went back to—not normal, how could it?—but at least back to how it'd been before. Hard work, not enough sleep, not enough food, not enough of anything 'cept whiskey and beatings. I didn't mind the work so much now. It kept me from thinking about Tom and what Papa and me done to him and his family. It hurt me inside when I thought about him in prison, he'd loved the outdoors so. And it hurt real bad to think about his wife, Helen, and their children. The pain I felt wasn't nothing against what they was going through. They hadn't done nothing to deserve this. The only reason this had happened was because a kind man had stopped one day to help me, a Ewell. It was all on account of me, and I was sure they couldn't hate me as much as I hated myself then.

If I was outside and seen his wife coming down the road, I'd duck into the cabin real quick till she'd went by. I watched for her the same way I'd once watched for Tom. Only now it was from guilt and shame.

Papa couldn't stop talking about how good he'd did in court. How he'd showed that snotty Mr. Finch and Judge Taylor and all the town folks. *Now* he reckoned they all knowed better than to take on Bob Ewell. It was positively a crime the way they had treated a hard-workin', Christian man like him, a poor widow-man who had to raise his family all by hisself. Well, he wasn't called upon to take that kind of disrespect. Nossir, they'd be right sorry someday. He'd show'em. He'd show'em all.

I got to where's I just wouldn't listen to him no more. Mostly he was drunk when he said these things, and I figured he wouldn't call them to mind after he sobered up.

But I did start to fret a little when I heard tell of a run-in he'd had with Mr. Finch the day after the trial. I never heard exactly what Papa said or done to Mr. Finch, but I knowed it was probably ugly, and I'm sure Papa come off looking mighty poor.

Mr. Finch had saw right through me and all my lies in court. He'd made me cry in front of everybody. But I didn't think he deserved the kind of trouble I knowed Papa could give him. I hoped, for his sake and his family's, that he'd steer clear of Papa for a while, long enough for him to simmer down and take his anger out on somebody else—like his family.

Trouble was, Papa never did simmer down.

He started in drinking more and more. Sometimes he'd lay up in bed screaming to me that *there was snakes, Mayella! snakes ever'where's and they're gonna get me sure!* When he got this way, I'd give him more whiskey till he got quiet enough to pass out. Other times, he'd go off in the woods and we wouldn't see him for days. I half-expected to see the sheriff show up some day and tell me that Papa was dead, or had done some horrible crime.

But worst of all was the fires. There begun to be fires down at the settlement. Always at night. Thank God, they was discovered and put out quick, and no one was hurt. I hoped they was just accidents, that it wasn't Papa'd been doing it. That'd be all we needed, for him to go to jail. As if the Ewells could sink any lower into the dirt.

After a couple weeks of this, the idea come to me that I oughta somehow get word to Mr. Finch about what Papa was doing. Maybe he could do something to stop Papa before someone got bad hurt. I didn't know exactly how to go about it, and I sure didn't want Papa to know what I was doing. I finally decided I'd write a letter and slip it under Mr. Finch's door at the courthouse. I was just beginning to write "For Mr. Finch," when I heard Papa coming in. I folded the note up quick and tucked it into my shift.

Papa busted into the cabin, and I could see he was near beside hisself.

"The bastard's dead! Had it comin' too, the goddam shine. Take on a Ewell, and see what it gits you! Saved the state some 'lectricity too! Haw, haw, haw!"

He stopped whooping and hollering long enough to give me the news.

Tom Robinson was dead. He'd been shot by the guards at the prison.

Papa commenced to carry on some more. He was most dancing with excitement.

"This is too good to keep to m'self, Mayella. I gotta go'n'share it with our goddam coon neighbors."

Then he was out the door, running down to the settlement. Pretty soon I heard him yelling and screaming his news at them.

I hadn't moved since he come in. I wanted to die. I wished the dirt under my feet would just open up and swaller me down.

Now I truly am a murderess, I told myself. I'd killed Tom Robinson same's if I had pulled the trigger myself.

I thought of the note I'd been writing. I took it out and held it in my hand and looked at it for a long time. And I was afraid. I was just too afraid. I tore the paper up into little pieces.

So in the end, I did nothing.

Chapter 21

Hiding Papa's Gun

After I heard that Tom was dead, I wanted to go and hide my wicked and shameful self, but there wasn't no place to go. I thought of him first thing in the morning when I got up, and last thing at night when I went to bed. I tried to pray, tried real hard, but I couldn't come up with any words that was right. I had been weak and wicked, and I knowed God didn't want to listen to me no more. I guess He finally seen what everybody else already knowed, that I was just another one of them Ewells. I didn't feel like Mama was ever near neither, not even when I touched her geraniums, the ones I had took such pains to grow back after they got stomped. I had shamed her so bad, and I was sure she didn't even want me as her daughter no more. I had failed at the good things I'd tried to do, poisoned the people I'd loved, and it was fitting now that I should feel completely alone. I felt like I was falling backwards into a black emptiness, never stopping, always falling. All's I could see was blackness behind me, in front of me, and me in the middle of it, lost, lost, always and forever.

So I just went through my days, doing my chores, cooking, washing, hauling water without really knowing I was doing them. The first time after Tom had died that Papa told me to bust up some kindling, I couldn't hardly see to chop. I thought I'd already cried all the tears I had, but still they come, spilling out of my eyes and blurring everything I seen.

It wasn't till near the end of October that I seen Papa was acting queerer than usual. Not just the drinking, but now I'd hear him talking to hisself a lot. He'd set on the porch, whiskey jug in hand, looking off towards the settlement, then back towards town, then mutter to hisself and laugh. One day I seen he had took his gun out. He set over it a goodly time, cleaning and polishing it. I didn't know but what the whiskey had made him crazy and I was afraid he might take it into his head and kill us and hisself some night. I decided that when I could, I'd take the gun and hide it somewheres that he couldn't get to it. Maybe I could get *that* much right.

I finally got the chance, I think it was a few days before Halloween. Papa was passed out as usual. I knowed where he kept the gun, so I snuck out with it and went a long ways off into the woods. Dug a hole and buried it deep. I made myself look around real good so's I'd remember where it was, case I ever needed it.

When Papa woke up and seen his gun was gone, he got crazy mad. He accused every one of us of having took it, but finally settled that it was Burris had did it. That was the only time I didn't step in between Papa and one of the children. I felt bad about it, but I just couldn't have Papa knowing what I done. He thrashed poor Burris till he was black and blue, and there wasn't nothing I could do, 'cept tend to his hurts when Papa was done.

Next day I seen Papa rooting through the dump. He musta thought his gun was in there, but no, he was after something else. My heart sunk when he pulled a knife outta there, a kitchen knife. That night he commenced to honing on it till it was real shiny and sharp, and I didn't like how his face looked one bit.

Well, I thought, *I'll have to make away with the knife like I done with the gun. Just have to watch and wait and see where he puts it away at.*

Thing was, he never did put it anywheres. He kept it with him all the time.

And then come Halloween.

Chapter 22

Halloween

Halloween was just another night to us Ewells. We never got no children begging candy or playing pranks out our way. And I sure wasn't scared of no haints. Papa was more than enough haint for me.

The night before, he'd tried to lay with me again, but this time was different. I fought. I fought back hard. I kicked out at him with all I had, and got him good in his—in his privates. He was pretty drunk, so I don't know how much it hurt him. But it sure did stop him. He layed on the floor, holding hisself and moaning. If he tried it again, I was gonna kick him again, and I think he knowed it too. After a time, he got up and staggered, all bent over, to his own bed and fell onto it with a groan.

He was my paw. Him and Mama had made me together, and we'd all been happy for a while. I remembered a time when he was kind and loved us, but them days was all gone now. I was glad I hurt him—it's awful to say it—but I was. I didn't care no more if he didn't come home for days on end. If he wanted to pass out on the floor and lay in his own filth, I let him. We was father and daughter, would always be, but I didn't care whether he lived or died. Mostly I wished him dead.

So that's how it was with me Halloween night. Papa was acting real twitchy as it got dark outside. He'd set down, then go look out the door, come back and set down again. Kept patting one of his pockets. Talked to hisself—I heard some words like "pay'im back twice't over," but I didn't know what he meant, and didn't think he did neither. He hadn't drank as much that night as he usually done, just enough to make him cantankerous and mouthy.

Finally he got up for the last time and when he got to the door, he turned around and said, "Lock up good'n'tight soon's I leave, Mayella. I might be out a while."

He closed the door, and I was just giving thanks for him being gone, when he stuck his head back in.

"And don't think I don't 'member about you kickin' me last night, you worthless slut. When I get back, you'll get the strap till you can't stand up no more."

Then he left for good.

I wasn't too fretted about the beating he'd promised. He'd most likely not remember when he sobered up. If he sobered up.

I don't know how long I'd been sleeping, nor even what time it was, when I woke up with a start. A car had pulled up in front of our cabin. Then I heard boot heels stepping soft on the porch. The children had woke up too and was scared, but I told them somebody must've give Papa a ride home from wherevers, and they should stay real quiet in bed.

The boot heels stopped, but Papa didn't come in.

Instead, there was a knock at the door. We never had no visitors during the day, much less the night, and I was plenty scared now, too. I crept outta my cot and grabbed up a good size piece of kindling. I walked slow and quiet to the door. Another knock.

Then a man's voice: "Miss Ewell? Miss Mayella Ewell?"

"Get away from here, we don't got nothin' for you to take!" I yelled.

"Miss Mayella? This here's Sheriff Heck Tate. Please open the door, ma'am, I got to talk to you. It's about your paw."

In jail, I thought. I knowed this was gonna happen. I opened the door and the sheriff come in. His face was awful grim, but he made his voice gentle when he spoke to me.

"Miss Mayella, I'm real sorry to have to tell you this, but—"

"Is Papa too drunk to come home? Did he do something bad? Just take him to jail, Sheriff, and I'll come collect him tomorrow."

"No, Miss Mayella, it ain't that at all. I'm real grieved to tell you this, ma'am, but he's dead. Your paw's dead."

PART 3

Chapter 23

Guilt

Papa had been dead near six months.

How he died, and what he was doing when he died, was so terrible I couldn't hardly bear to think of it.

Halloween night, he left our cabin with that new-honed kitchen knife tucked away in his pocket. He still beared Mr. Finch a grudge for showing him up in court, so he hunted down that man's two innocent children, hunted them like they was rabbits. My paw was gonna kill *children*, young'uns just like us. It made me sick all over to think about it.

Luckily, the boy fought back. Papa hurt him pretty bad, a broke arm, I think. The little girl was wearing a Halloween costume, and that saved her from Papa's knife.

Sheriff Tate told me that in their fight, Papa had fell on his own knife. It was a gut wound, deep, and he just bled out till he was dead.

After I had got over the first shock of the news, I got another. I was happy and grateful that he was dead and couldn't hurt none of us no more. To try to kill little children like that, he deserved to die, and it was fitting that he ended up killing his own self. It was right. Papa had made me hate him for so many things, for so many years, that I didn't have no more feelings for him. I tried to at least pray for his soul, but all's I could think was, *Thank You, God. Thank You, God.*

And what if I hadn't took away his gun and hid it? He would for certain have killed them, and then mighta come back for the four of us, too.

Like when Mama passed, I didn't know what to do about Papa's body and the burial. I didn't know where any of Papa's family was. The sheriff asked Miss Ruth from the welfare office to come out and get things arranged for me. I was grateful for that. She told me not to fret, that she would get everything took care of.

There was just three of us children at Papa's burying. Me, Sally, and Elias. Soon as Burris heard Papa was dead, he had took off into the woods, and didn't come back. To this day, I don't know if it was because I had slapped him that time, or Papa's beatings. Partly I think it was because he hadn't never gotten over Mama's death real good. Turned out, we wouldn't never see him again.

With the burying over, I had time to set and think a while about things. I was glad Papa wasn't with us no more, but the feeling come to me stronger and stronger, that it had been me, really, that had set everything off.

I had wished for a friend. That friend had been a Negro. I had invited him to come into our yard, and into our cabin. I had loved him. After Papa made me lay with him, then seen me with Tom the next day, he'd went to the sheriff, and got Tom arrested. Papa had made me lie and both of us come off looking real bad at the trial, but it didn't matter. Tom was found guilty and sent to prison. He was shot and killed later by some guards.

The death of one innocent man wasn't enough for Papa, though. He had never stopped hating Mr. Finch, had never stopped thinking of a way to get back at him. Papa was a coward, and he went to get his revenge by killing Mr. Finch's children.

So you see, *I* was the bad one, *I* was to blame for Tom's death. And even Papa's. And if Papa had killed Mr. Finch's children, that woulda been my fault too. I was the guilty one, and what made it worse was that I still lived, when the others had not.

The black hole I'd felt myself falling into ever since Tom Robinson died was only getting blacker and deeper.

Chapter 24

Giving Up

In the time since Papa had killed hisself, things had went from bad to worse. Everything was on my shoulders now, and I'd never felt weaker. I couldn't hardly keep up with the chores or make sure that Sally and Elias was took good care of. I tried to find out where Burris might have went to, but I give up on that after a while. I was just so tired, tired all the time, even though I was sleeping longer and longer into the mornings. During the day, I'd either cry, or set in one spot for hours, staring at nothing, feeling numb. I didn't have no appetite, so I give my share of what food we had to the children. I give up trying to keep myself clean. Just let my greasy hair hang in strings. I couldn't face hauling enough water for a bath, so I let that go, too.

Things went on this way for a long time. I was just falling deeper and deeper down that black hole. I knowed it would have me and swaller me in the end.

One night, I made a decision. I don't know why I hadn't thought of it before. The children couldn't live with me like this no more. It wasn't no fair to them. They was still young and had a chance of a life.

So I went into town the next morning and called Aunt Pansy. She showed she still had every bit as big a heart as ever. Yes, she'd be glad to take Sally and Elias into her home—

there was always room for more, she said. And room for me too if I wanted. I couldn't hardly thank her proper for crying. Just keep'em for a little while, I told her, till I could get things going better here. It wouldn't be long, I promised.

Aunt Pansy come the very next day, and it felt so much like that other time she had came, when Mama had just died. Sally and Elias was real excited about going in a car and that made it easier to say goodbye to them.

Just before they drove off, Aunt Pansy run her car window down.

"What about you, Mayella? You sure you're gonna be all right? How're you gonna feed yourself, honey?"

I don't know why I done it, but I thought real quick and made up a story. Oh, she wasn't to worry about me, I said, I just got me a job down to the OK Café in town. It'll bring in some money, and I'll save up till I can get the children back with me.

I'm not sure she believed me. She looked me over, from my filthy hair to my ragged shift, and only said, "You need anything, you just call, honey, all right? Promise?"

I promised. We waved and blowed kisses till they was outta sight.

*   *   *

It was about a week after the children had went with Aunt Pansy that the food begun to show up.

I'd get up in the morning, and there'd be some fried chicken and some biscuit left on the porch. Or I'd come back from hauling water, and a plate of ham might be setting there. Once even some peach pickles and a cake.

The first time I seen the food setting there, it hit me wrong. I got mad. I picked up the bowl and throwed it across the yard and into the dump. "I don't need no pity from any of you people!" I'd shouted. I felt like I was going crazy. But the food kept coming anyway. Then I was ashamed of how

I'd acted, and tried to be thankful that somebody was looking out for me. But who was bringing it?

Didn't they know I wasn't worth it? Didn't they know I was a Ewell?

'Bout the only time I stepped outside now was to take in the plates of food. I didn't want to be looked at or gossiped about by Maycomb folks. I wasn't worth their gossip neither.

So I stayed there alone in the cabin with only my own pitiful thoughts for company. And that deep, black hole. That never left me. Everybody else had, but not it. It was my only company, my only friend now. Mama had told me once that me, by myself, would always be enough. But I knowed now that wasn't true. Me, by myself, wasn't nothing.

One day, I finally come to a point where I knowed two things for sure. Only two, but they was real important.

The first was that I wanted to be with my mama.

And the other was that I remembered where I'd buried Papa's gun.

Chapter 25

Mama's Voice

The only thing I could find to dig with was the ax. It seemed fitting somehow to use the ax that Tom had touched to do what I had to do.

I found the place without hardly any trouble. The ground was dry, and I had to chop hard at the dirt. No time at all, I had the gun and carried it back to the cabin.

I had been gone maybe twenty minutes all together, but in that time, somebody had left another plate of food on the porch. I didn't even look to see what it was, because I knowed I wouldn't be eating it. But I thanked the person in my mind, and was glad they wouldn't have the trouble of doing it no more.

I stood on the porch and looked all around me. At the dump where Mama had took my first and only dress out of, and where Papa had found the kitchen knife. Mama's geraniums was setting proud in the warm sunlight. I seen the stump that I had chopped kindling on. Where I had fell with the ax and heard Tom's voice for the first time. I looked up at the cabin roof, where Mama and Papa and us children would sometimes set on hot nights and be a family. I said goodbye to everything I ever seen and knowed. One last moment in the sunshine for me, then I went inside and shut the door.

I set down on my cot. Shouldn't be too hard to figure out how to work the gun. I cleaned all the dirt and grit outta it, then opened it to make sure there was bullets. There was.

Almost ready, but I still had some things to do yet.

I wrote a note to Aunt Pansy, telling her how sorry I was that I couldn't never take the children back. I knowed she'd raise them just like Mama had did us. Told her I just couldn't be no good to any of them now, and they wasn't to fret about me no more. I was in a better place.

I put the note on the kitchen table.

Next, I kneeled down by Mama's cot and prayed. This time, the words *did* come: *Thank You for the happy times I had when I was little. Thank You for giving me such a good mama. Thank You for letting me have Tom Robinson for a friend. Please ask both of them to forgive me for the horrible things I done, though I know I ain't worthy of it. And please, God, please forgive me, too. Only You knowed what was in my heart the whole time. Thank You for letting it finally be over, and please let it be quick.*

One last thing, then it'd be time.

I got another piece of paper and wrote on it:

Mayella Violet Ewell, Her Will

I leave everything I have to Helen Robinson, because it was me that took away everything she had.

There. That was the last of it.

I layed on the cot and put the gun to my head. Started to tighten down on the trigger.

"*Mayella.*"

I sat up. Who'd called me?

"*Mayella.*" The voice was so soft, I couldn't hardly make it out, but it sounded to me just like—like—

"Mama? Mama? Oh, God, where are you, Mama?"

Because it was my own mama's voice—coming from where—inside my head? My heart? I heard it louder and clearer now.

"*Don't do this, honey. Who'll take care of my geraniums now, Mayella, if you die, my child, my good dau—*"

Her voice trailed away.

"Mama! Oh Mama, please let me see you. Please tell me what to do. Help me, Mama! Help me!"

And somehow, she did.

* * *

It took every bit of strength I had to walk to town. I was pretty sure I knowed where I was going, but didn't know what to do once I got there. I fetched up in front of his house, and walked to the door. My legs was shaking something awful. I had to knock twice before someone opened it.

It was a colored lady.

"Please, ma'am, c'n I see Mr. Finch?"

Seemed like forever, but suddenly he was standing in front of me, looking surprised but friendly at me.

"Why, Miss Mayella, whatever—is there anything I can help you with?"

I couldn't speak. My mouth was moving, but no words come out. I was shaking all over.

"Child, what is it?"

The words busted outta me like a flood.

"Mr. Finch, my mama spoke to me—she sent me to you, for certain she did—can you please help me not to die? Please help me, Mr. Finch, you know what I—*Oh God, forgive me for what I done!* God forgive me! Help me not to die, Mr. Finch!"

After that, the deep, black hole got me at last and I hit the bottom. I didn't know no more.

Chapter 26

Saved

I woke up from the darkness and heard voices coming from somewheres above me. Felt somebody holding on to my wrist. A cool cloth was on my forehead, and I was laying, not on a dirt floor, but a settee. I was scared to open my eyes because I was starting to remember where I was and how I'd got there. I felt weak and near dead, but finally I did look, and I seen Mr. Finch and another man standing over me. The man was telling Mr. Finch that my pulse was near normal again. *He must be a doctor!* I thought. *A real doctor!* I'd never saw nor been tended to by one in my whole life.

"Well, Mr. Finch, she's coming around now nicely, and I'll leave her in your good hands. Call me if she needs anything further."

The doctor left, and Mr. Finch pulled up a chair while I tried to set up. My arms couldn't hardly hold me up.

"Gently, child, gently. Wait until you feel stronger."

"What—what happened to me?" I asked.

"You fainted, Miss Mayella. Fainted dead away right on my doorstep. Do you remember anything about it?"

His voice was kind, but when I heard him say "dead," everything all come back to me in a rush. I begun to cry, hard, choking sobs that I thought wouldn't never stop. I tried to hide my guilty, shamed face with my hands. I heard him say some comforting things, then he tucked a handkerchief into my hands. After a bit, I was some calmer.

"Mr. Finch, I come here to—to apologize to you, sir, for everything my family has done to your'n."

He waited for me to go on.

"Papa'd never'a done it if it wasn't for me. It was all my fault, sir. Tom Robinson was my friend, *he* never raped or beat me, I lied 'bout all them things because—I was so scared. And if I'd only told the truth, none of this would ever have happened. It's my fault, Mr. Finch, and I want to, I have to, make things right with y'all somehow."

"I know, my child. I understand. You were forced to lie because you were frightened of what your father would do to you. And I know that—that father of yours was the one who did beat and rape you."

I nodded. I couldn't speak for the tears. Thank God somebody finally knowed what really happened.

"It's a mercy, child, that you weren't—that you didn't become—well, I'm just glad that you survived such an unspeakable ordeal. Most women would not have. I think you must have a great deal of inner strength, and I admire that in you."

"Mr. Finch, I was led to your house—my mama told me to come—I don't know how, but she did. And it feels so good to say the truth at last. So now you can do anything you want to me, sir, I know I deserve it and worse."

"The only thing I want to do is get some food into you, child. Goodness, you're almost skin and bones. How long has it been since you've eaten?"

"I don't rightly recollect, sir."

He asked the colored woman—her name was Miss Calpurnia—to fix me up with some food. She took me into the kitchen with her while she done it. I never seen such a clean place in all my days. She had me to set down at the table, and she put a plate down in front of me—oh my! There was so much food on it, I didn't think I'd be able to eat it all, but it seemed like the more I ate, the hungrier I got. When it was all gone, I remembered, too late, that I shoulda said thanks over it. I bent my head down to pray, and that's when I noticed the color and pattern of the plate. *I knowed that plate.* Knowed it real well—seen it many times setting on the porch of the cabin, piled high with food for me.

Here I'd come to this house to confess about my lies and be punished, and instead, they had took me in, called a doctor for me, and fed me. I felt like I was in Heaven. I wondered if this was how regular folks do all the time?

Mr. Finch stepped into the kitchen to ask kindly if I would please come back into the living room with him. He stayed standing till I got set down, then he set too.

"Miss Mayella," he asked, "Do you feel well enough to tell me everything you can about what has happened to you?"

I said I'd try. I didn't know where to begin, but I begun with Mama's death and told him everything, like he asked.

It took a long time for me to get through it, and I was afraid he'd get tired of listening. But his eyes never left my face, and I knowed he was hearing every word.

When I was done, he set there a while. He said not to fret, he was just thinking. After a time, he reached over and took my hand. I pulled back at first, I felt so dirty, but he held on all the tighter. He asked me to look at him, and I did, though I felt real shy.

"I want to tell you something, Miss Mayella, and I want you to remember this always. *You are not your father.* You never made him do anything. He did all those things to himself. And you, your mother, and your brothers and sisters were cruelly victimized by him. None of this had anything to do with you. You are not your father, and I want you to know that *I* know that, too. If anyone should take any of the blame, it is I, because I ought to have looked into your living arrangements after your mother died. So please don't take on all the guilt yourself, my dear."

He stopped and shook his head like he was sad, and went on.

"You were just another one of the innocents, my poor child."

I tried to speak, to say how thankful and grateful I was, but I was crying too hard. His words had went straight into my heart, into my soul, and I had never felt so comfortable in my life.

"I am so sorry that you had to go through all this. And it's my fervent hope that your life from this moment on will be a much happier and safer one. I will see to that, if you will let me."

I told him I didn't have no words big enough to thank him for his kindness to me, and that I wished my mama was still alive to see this.

"Miss Mayella, you are a pure and innocent child. You have a tender heart, and I know this from the way you took such good care of your mother in her final days. Poor soul. You truly were *her good daughter.*"

A chill went through me like a knife when he said that, and I felt like I might faint again.

I never thought to hear those words ever again, and I knowed right there and then that Mama was speaking to me again, speaking across the long reach of Heaven, through good Mr. Finch.

Chapter 27

Miss Maudie's Idea

My life after that become different as night and day.

When I got strong enough, Mr. Finch asked his neighbor lady, Miss Atkinson, if I could board with her for a time. I'm sure he must've told her everything about me, and she knowed I was a Ewell, but she took me in anyways, and made me feel as welcome as if I'd been, well, anybody else. I don't think I have ever knowed so many good folks all at once and in the same place.

Living in her house now, I had light, warmth, quiet, cleanness. A wood floor, not a dirt one. A real dress and real shoes. Always enough to eat. No more hollering and stomping, no more beatings, no more drunkenness. The only times I felt sad was when I wished Mama could be in this new life with me, or that Tom could be alive again.

Near every morning, I'd wake up and wonder how in the world I had ended up here. Then I'd remember, and I would close my eyes and pray to God to bless these good people, these good angels, for taking me in and giving me shelter.

Miss Atkinson went back to the cabin with me to help me pack some things. I wouldn't be living there no more. I didn't hardly have anything much to take, but I did want the dress Mama had made over for me, the box of her hairpins, and, of course, her geraniums. Miss Atkinson said she never seen such beautiful flowers, and I was proud to tell her that they was my mama's, and that she had passed them on to me. I took the note I'd left for Aunt Pansy and tore it up. The gun was still laying on the bed. Miss Atkinson said that Mr. Finch would come later and take care of it. I also took the will I had wrote. I would ask Mr. Finch if he could fix it so's it'd be all legal.

It was dark as ever in the cabin, and when we come outta there for the last time, I seen tears in Miss Atkinson's eyes. I asked her what was the matter? She started to say, "Child, did you *really*—" but stopped herself and then allowed as how her eyes was just weak and watery from the dust.

I stayed with her for most three months. During that time, she fed me up to where I got my weight back. I didn't realize how much strength I had lost after Papa died. Sometimes Miss Calpurnia would come over and the two of them would help me with my reading, writing, and numbers. I'd got a little backward over the years, but they was good teachers, and it didn't take long for me to get cotched up. They also taught me how to cook real simple but good meals. Showed me how to keep a house clean and neat. How to sew for myself and others. Dr. Reynolds—the doctor that had tended to me the day I fainted at Mr. Finch's door—come over, too, and he taught me how to nurse and care for sick people. He said I had a real knack for it, and that it was a good thing to know how to do.

I just couldn't get over how nice all them folks was to me. I told Miss Atkinson over and over again that I wished there was something I could do to pay them back for all they done for me.

She set there for a spell and thought.

Then she said, "Maybe you can, Mayella. I've an idea that I need to discuss with Mr. Finch."

Chapter 28

A Chance to Heal

It was a day or two later, I guess, when she asked me to go with her over to Mr. Finch's house. When we got there, Mr. Finch and Dr. Reynolds was setting on the porch. They both stood up when they seen us come up the sidewalk.

Mr. Finch spoke first.

"Please, sit down, ladies. Well, Miss Mayella, I hear from Miss Maudie and the good doctor here that you have developed a real talent for nursing, and that you have also become quite a good housekeeper and cook. I'm very proud of you, my child. But I'm not surprised. I was certain that you had a good head and heart in you."

I turned red. I still wasn't used to hearing nice things spoke about me, but I knowed I'd *never* get tired of him calling me his child.

"Thank you, sir, but it's really Miss Atkinson, and Doctor Reynolds and Miss Calpurnia, and you, Mr. Finch, that's—"

I stopped speaking as his face looked serious all of a sudden.

"Have you thought, child, about what you would like to do, what sort of job you might work at, so that you can one day become independent?"

I said I had, lots of times, and what did he think of me working as a waitress at the OK Café?

He laughed gently and shook his head.

"Well, the three of us think we might know of something else you could do that would be a bit more, shall we say, rewarding, Miss Mayella. This job we are thinking of would require all those useful skills you have been acquiring."

"I'll do anything y'all ask of me, sir. Anything. Just tell me what it is, please."

He said that there was a man they all knowed who was very sick. His brother couldn't take care of him no more, and he needed someone to look after him.

"He has an illness called tuberculosis, Miss Mayella. That's a disease of the lungs. It makes him very weak, and not able to speak much. He has to stay in bed a great deal of the time, and he never goes out, at least not since—well, he just doesn't go out anymore. Dr. Reynolds says that his prognosis is poor—that is, he will eventually die. It may not happen for several years yet. But in time, the sickness will simply wear his poor body out."

I thought of Mama, and of how she had went the same way. Mr. Finch went on.

"Dr. Reynolds would take care of the more complicated medical tasks. What you would do is to keep house for him, cook his meals and bring them to him, and do some simple nursing. This man—he did my family a great service once, Miss Mayella, and I would like to see him live out his remaining years in as much comfort and ease as possible. Would you be willing to move into his house and take care of him?"

Miss Atkinson cleared her throat. She muttered something to Mr. Finch. I could hear what her words, but I didn't know what they meant.

"Atticus, are you going to tell her—"

"No," he said. "She won't ever need to know *that*."

He turned to me again.

"What do you think, my dear? Will you do this for us, and for him?"

"If you think I can do it, Mr. Finch, I will. I took care of Mama, you know, when she—If you think I can help this poor man, I would try real hard not to let y'all down."

"You could never let us down, Miss Mayella. I have complete confidence and trust that you will do all you can to help our friend."

"Thank you, sir. I thank all of y'all, with all my heart and soul. You don't know, you can't know, how you have saved me, and give me back my life."

"Everyone is worth saving, Miss Mayella, and I'm glad that you will now help us to save Mr. Arthur."

"I will, sir. And Mr. Finch? Thank you. Thank you for calling me 'Miss' Mayella."

Chapter 29

Path to Redemption

Yesterday Mr. Finch took me to where Tom Robinson is buried and I planted one of Mama's geraniums on it. Geraniums are for comfort, and I hope Tom's family will know what I'm trying to say. As we was leaving, I asked Mr. Finch if he thought Tom and his family would ever forgive me.

"Child," he said, "I think that in order for us to feel forgiven, we must learn to try and forgive ourselves first."

Now I know what to pray for.

* * *

I met him for the first time yesterday, and will move into his house in a few days. I was a little timid of him at first, and I think he was of me, too. When Mr. Finch said who I was, Mr. Arthur ducked his head, then raised his eyes to Mr. Finch like he was asking a question. Mr. Finch didn't say nothing, just shook his head a little. Then Mr. Arthur's eyes met mine, and I seen right away that he couldn't never even hurt a fly. His eyes are kind and gentle, like Mr. Finch's. Like Tom's.

To know such men like them—it's like Mama sent them to me special, to show me that there are real good people like that in this world. She was right. If a man is good inside, it will show on the outside.

I'm also a little scared I might fail and let them down, but I have faith that the good angels God has sent to me are putting me in the place I need to be. By helping Mr. Arthur, I hope I can start to get my soul back, piece by piece. To learn to forgive myself. And to get what I need so's I can see my mama again someday:

Redemption.

EPILOGUE

He knows what people in this town think about him and his family. They call him a haint, a leering, drooling monster that eats cats and squirrels. He sees folks break into a run as they go past his sad house, or start whistling to keep the phantom away. They think he was locked in here because he stabbed his father, and that if he's not already dead, he's been driven crazy in his forced solitude.

But they forget.

There was a time when he walked in the world beside them. No, he never walked—he ran, ran for the sake of feeling the wind in his face, hearing his blood race and sing in his veins, his breath keeping time with his pounding heart. He swam under a full moon in Barker's Eddy; he drank till he was tipsy; played poker till he lost all his pocket money; and he danced with girls who weren't afraid to let their young, ripening bodies touch his.

Now his world is one of endless shadows and dim twilights, and as he watches the Outside ones and their world from behind dusty, tattered curtains, he wonders—is he the ghost, or are they?

He never goes out of his bedroom now. He knows that there is a time coming when he will leave his room and his house, and be Outside, never to return. But he also knows that there is one coming to help ease him into that transition. He and she are inextricably linked forever, but she will never know in what way. She will bring her loving heart, her wounded soul, and her geraniums, and she will help him turn from ghost into pure Spirit.

And he feels comforted.

223

BVG